Chasing Forever

A Sweet Escapes Novel

Susan Coventry

Chasing Forever Copyright © 2019 by Susan Coventry. All Rights Reserved.

All rights reserved. No part of this book may be reproduced in any form or by any electronic or mechanical means including information storage and retrieval systems, without permission in writing from the author. The only exception is by a reviewer, who may quote short excerpts in a review.

Cover designed by Woodchuck Arts
Cover photo: iStock Photo

This book is a work of fiction. Names, characters, places, and incidents either are products of the author's imagination or are used fictitiously. Any resemblance to actual persons, living or dead, events, or locales is entirely coincidental.

Susan Coventry
Visit my website at www.susancoventry.org

Printed in the United States of America

First Printing: May 2019
Coventry Industries LLC

ISBN: 9781097166848

Also by Susan Coventry

A New Chapter
An Island Christmas Wedding
Anything For You
Better Than Fiction
Capture The Moment
Custom Built for Me
Love Notes
Me & You Plus Two
Right Here With You
See You Then
Starring You and Me
The Perfect Distraction
The Perfect Gentleman
The Perfect Blend
The Sweetest Mistake
Twice as Tempting

Prologue

Dear Callie,

If you're reading this, I've already joined your grandpa in heaven. At least, I hope he's there. He did swear a lot while he was alive. Anyway, I know you're probably sad right now, but please don't cry for me. I've missed the old fart for the past few years, and I'm happy to be reunited with him again.

By now, you've had to suffer through my funeral and sorting through all my junk, but here comes the good part. A few weeks ago, when I realized I didn't have much time left, I booked a trip for you. I hope you're not upset with me, but even if you are, you'll get over it when I tell you where.

Remember that resort we stayed at on Kauai that time the whole family went? Well, I took the liberty of booking the same condo for you for eight weeks, starting on the first of February. I wish I could see your face right now to know if you're mad, elated, or somewhere in between. But hear me out.

Susan Coventry

I know what a rough year you've had with my illness and that idiot breaking up with you. I also know that you put your writing on hold because of me. You sat at my bedside day after day, and you never complained. But now that I'm gone, you have to get back to it, Callie.

Writing is in your blood. It's something you were always meant to do. Some of my greatest joy these past few years came from reading your books. I was so proud of you. Did I tell you that enough? I certainly hope so. Anyway, I hate to think that your "dry spell" was because of me, though I know I'm partially to blame. I'm sorry for what I put you through, and I wanted to make it up to you.

You may be thinking this is going above and beyond a grandma's duty, but you're wrong. The condo on Kauai is already paid for. All you have to do is book a flight, and you're on your way. (I figured the money I left you will help with that and your other expenses.)

Here's what I want you to do. I want you to go to Hawaii, relax your mind, and get your mojo back. Isn't that what they call it? Forget all about that idiot and what you've been through this past year and pick up your pen again. I wouldn't have booked the place if I didn't think you could do it. I know you still have a lot of stories left to tell, and the world needs to hear them.

I hope you're not shaking your head right now or coming up with a zillion excuses why you shouldn't go. There are none! You're a writer. You can work anywhere, and why not Hawaii, one of the most romantic places on earth?

This will be the last time your old grandma tells you what to do, so humor me. Take your laptop, notepads, and pens and escape for eight weeks. Even if you return without a story (which I doubt), you'll have a great tan and, hopefully, a clearer head.

I love you, sweetie. You've always brought me such joy since the time you were a tiny baby. Now it's my turn to give something back. Take the trip and know that I'll be smiling down on you and awaiting your next great romance book.

Do you think people read in heaven? I certainly hope so!
Love, hugs, and kisses,
Grandma Cooper

Chapter 1

Aloha! Callie heard the cheerful greeting everywhere as she walked through the airport, bought herself a bagel and coffee, and picked up a red Jeep Wrangler at the car rental agency.

The people are all so friendly here, and no wonder! She'd forgotten how stunningly beautiful Hawaii was. The last time she'd been there, she'd been a college student on spring break. Her parents had splurged for plane fare for her and her best friend, and they'd met up with her grandparents, two aunts and uncles, and a handful of cousins. They'd rented a block of condos on the tranquil island of Kauai and had a blast swimming, snorkeling, and exploring the beautiful beaches and quaint towns. She remembered thinking she wanted to return there someday, but the years had passed, and it had become a distant memory—until now.

Chasing Forever

If only her reason for being there hadn't been prompted by her grandma's death. She fought back tears as she thought about her grandma's letter and all that had transpired over the past year. Her grandma, Irene, had been diagnosed with lung cancer, and it had been shocking since she had never smoked a day in her life. "Something had to get me," Irene had bravely said after hearing the diagnosis.

Since losing her husband a few years ago, she'd talked about wanting to join him in heaven, but Callie had dismissed it as a joke. Irene was too spry and feisty to die yet, and Callie wasn't ready to let her go. They'd always been close, and Callie credited Irene for her decision to become a writer. Irene had loved reading, and she'd passed it along to Callie. She had fond memories of sitting on her grandma's lap as Irene read aloud, adopting different accents for each character in the book and making the story come alive.

From a young age, Callie had answered the question "What do you want to be when you grow up?" with "A writer." And she hadn't veered from it. In fact, as she'd gotten older, the idea had taken root in her brain and wouldn't let go. Even when her parents had warned that she might not make much money (unlike James Patterson, J.K. Rowling, and the like), she'd dug in her heels. "It's not about the money. It's about following my passion," she'd argued. "I don't want to take some boring desk job just because it provides a steady paycheck."

Her dad had shaken his head and said, "This is all your grandmother's doing." But it looked like he'd been trying to hide a smile, and Callie had noticed. So, she'd gone to college, earned an English degree, and followed her dream.

After college, she'd churned out a few novels per year until she had a successful romance series. Then suddenly she lost her mojo (as her grandma so eloquently put it). It had started when her long-term boyfriend, Adam, had broken up with her. She hadn't realized how important a loving relationship was to a romance writer until he left. Not that everything had been perfect, but their relationship had provided plenty of inspiration, especially when it came to writing sex scenes.

While her books weren't autobiographical, there might have been a few similarities. For example, when she wrote about falling in love, she'd recall the emotions she'd experienced with Adam. That initial excitement, anticipation, desire, and angst—she'd written about it all, assigning her emotions to fictional characters.

Even their arguments had provided useful fodder, including the little disappointments that arose over time. In addition to having her own muse, she'd also drawn on her friends' relationships. For seven years, she'd had plenty of material to work with, and then everything changed.

Adam graduated with a degree in finance and was working his way up as a loan officer in a major bank. As his responsibilities increased, so did his hours. The more time he spent at the bank and the less they spent together caused a tear in their relationship. It was barely noticeable at first, just a general feeling of disappointment whenever he came home late or missed dinner. But soon the disappointments turned into arguments, and the tear increased.

Oddly, she'd never suspected there might be another reason he'd been spending so much time at work. How could she have been so blind? She was a romance writer, for Pete's sake! She wrote about this stuff all the time.

She'd never forget the day she'd figured it out. After college, Adam had moved into her apartment near campus. Since she stayed home writing and he was gone all day, she'd occasionally do his laundry. Generally, she believed they were equal partners and should take care of their own laundry, but one Friday evening when he was working late, she decided to put in a load for him.

She'd been sorting through his dirty clothes basket, feeling in pockets for anything he might have inadvertently left there, when she came across a restaurant receipt. Ordinarily, she wouldn't have been surprised, since Adam often went out to lunch with his co-workers. But there were two things that tipped her off.

First, the receipt was for a new Mexican restaurant that had recently opened near his office. She'd been asking to go there for a few weeks since they were both fans of Mexican food. He'd kept putting her off since he'd been working late most nights, and afterward he just wanted to come home. Never once had he mentioned that he'd already gone there. Secondly, the time and date on the receipt rang a bell. He'd gone there the previous Friday evening at 6:30 p.m., after he'd called and said he had to stay late and finish a report for his boss. That night, he hadn't come home until nine o'clock.

She'd been lying on the couch, watching a romantic movie (for research purposes) when he'd walked in. But instead of coming over to kiss her, he'd said a quick hello and immediately gone into their bedroom to change. When he came back out to join her, he complained about being exhausted, and she sat there and listened, none the wiser. She recalled asking if he'd had time to eat dinner, and he said he'd eaten a leftover sandwich at his desk.

Chasing Forever

How stupid could she be? Never once in their relationship had he given her reason to distrust him, but after finding that receipt, she'd questioned everything. The months of him working late, the lessening of their sex life, his lack of interest in her writing. It all made sense now. She'd partially blamed herself for being so caught up in her "fictional world" that she hadn't paid enough attention to her real relationship. If she had, she might have been able to salvage it.

But, when she'd lamented to her best friend, Quinn, she had set her straight. "It's not your fault, Callie. It's his. The asshole should have been honest with you instead of sneaking around behind your back."

When she'd confronted Adam later that evening, he hadn't denied it. Soon it all came pouring out. *She* was a bank teller who had been working there for six months. It had started as a harmless flirtation (yeah, right!) and then had progressed into more (read: sex). He was extremely sorry and had been contemplating when and how to tell her, but she'd saved him the trouble. All because she'd been nice enough to do his laundry! She'd never make that mistake again!

After the shedding of tears (hers) and the hurling of insults (also hers), they'd parted ways. That night, he'd packed his bags (he was a minimalist, so there hadn't been many) and left, presumably to go to *her* house.

Once he'd walked out the door, Callie realized he'd never said the woman's name. Had that been on purpose? Had he worried she might go into the bank, seek out the woman, and confront her in front of his co-workers? For a few minutes, she considered it. Surely, the bank didn't condone office relationships unless they were more modern than she'd thought. Come to think of it, she hadn't asked much about Adam's job, and she kicked herself again for being too caught up in "her stories" to pay attention.

So, while she'd been heartbroken, she also accepted her share of the blame for their break-up. Still, it hadn't made it easier to take that she'd become like one of the characters in her books who'd been shoved aside for another woman.

"Channel it into your writing," Quinn had suggested. "Make him an evil character who gets killed off in the end. That'll teach him!"

Callie had laughed. "I can't do that. I write romance not horror stories. Besides, romance readers expect a happy ending."

"You can still have your happy ending, Callie. It just won't include Adam."

But how do you get over a seven-year relationship that easily? It felt impossible, and as Callie had marinated in her grief, she'd neglected her writing. She'd kept thinking, *I'll get back to it in a few days*, but then it became a few weeks, and soon it had been a few months since she'd written a word. It wasn't from lack of trying. She'd sat in front of her laptop every day at her usual start time of 8 a.m. and waited for the words to come. But they'd alluded her. She'd start a sentence and then delete it. She'd done it so many times that she'd finally given up and decided to take a break. And then the unthinkable had happened—her grandma had been diagnosed with cancer.

Now, as she rumbled down the two-lane road leading to the resort, she remembered that day like it was yesterday. Callie had taken Irene for her annual physical like she'd insisted on doing ever since her grandpa had died. Irene was still capable of driving and reminded her of that every time, but Callie was stubborn (she'd learned that from her grandma). Irene was eighty-two years old, and Callie wanted to soak up whatever amount of time they had left together. Besides, after the appointment, they always went out to lunch and sometimes shopping, so she hadn't minded at all.

Callie had been sitting in the waiting room, reading a steamy romance on her Kindle (for pleasure and research purposes), when Irene had come out with a disgruntled expression on her face.

"What's wrong?" Callie had asked immediately.

"Not here," Irene had replied.

Once they were inside the car, Irene explained what had happened. One week prior to her physical, she'd had a chest x-ray that showed a suspicious spot on her right lung. The doctor had discussed the results with her and referred her to a cancer specialist. Callie sat in shock while the words sank in. Her beloved grandma, the woman who was perhaps her greatest inspiration, might have cancer.

While they'd been sitting there, Irene had clasped Callie's hand to provide comfort when it should have been the other way around. When Callie had started crying, Irene had gathered her close and said, "Cancer doesn't have to be a death sentence. Don't worry, sweetie. I'm not ready to kick off just yet."

But less than a year later, her grandma was gone, and now Callie was in Hawaii, one of the most beautiful places on earth—alone.

Chapter 2

Alone at last! Finally! After a shitty year, Chase Edwards was blissfully alone. He'd rolled into the resort earlier that morning, brought in his luggage, and collapsed on the couch, where he'd napped for two hours. Pure heaven. He woke up groggy yet happy and set about unpacking.

It was hard to believe he was going to be on Kauai for eight weeks, but all he had to do was look out the patio door to know it was real. He'd opened all the windows to the sights, sounds, and scents of the resort and the ocean beyond. It had been so long since he'd been on vacation he'd forgotten how soothing it could be.

It was a gorgeous February day—yes, February—and he was tempted to take pictures and send them to his buddies to gloat. When he'd left Michigan the day before, the temperature had been in the teens, and he'd had to sit on the plane for an extra hour while they'd de-iced it. The delay hadn't bothered him, though, because he'd be leaving the cold and all the other crap behind. By that, he meant the incident that had occurred just before Christmas.

The memory of that night was still crystal clear, and every time he recalled it; he'd become consumed with anger all over again. Chase had just left an appointment with a client, and he'd called his girlfriend, Cassandra, on his way home to see if she wanted him to bring Chinese. She hadn't answered, but a few minutes later, she'd texted that she was out with friends and he should eat without her.

He hadn't thought it unusual because, even though they were a couple, they both made time for their friends. He pictured her at a restaurant with her "girls," drinking girly drinks and giggling while they shared stories of their sex lives. Did women really do that? He wanted to think so, and he'd hoped Cass was sharing some good ones about them. If there was one area of his life he was a hundred percent confident in, it was his prowess in the sack.

He'd always been a good student, and not only in academics. He'd studied women too, learning almost everything he needed to know in his college years, when there'd been plenty of opportunities. His biggest takeaway—see to the woman's pleasure first, and then she'd be happy to see to his! It had been a lesson that had served him well, including with Cassandra (or so he'd thought).

In his business, there'd been no shortage of women, but none that knocked his socks off the way she had. She was gorgeous, with her strawberry blonde hair, legs for miles, and killer smile. When he'd first met her, he'd been surprised that she was single. But less than a year after they'd started dating, he'd figured out why.

Behind the killer smile, she was like a black widow spider, luring men into her web, pleasuring them, and then eating them alive.

Since he hadn't wanted to eat alone that night, he'd decided to drop in on his buddy Patrick, a lawyer from another firm in the Detroit area. Chase hadn't bothered calling first because it was Monday night, and he figured Patrick would be home drinking beer and watching football. During football season, he'd often get together with Patrick and a few other guys to do just that. So, Chase swung by his favorite Chinese place, picked up a few things he knew Patrick would like, and headed over to his house.

When he pulled into the driveway, he was glad to see a light on, which meant Patrick was home. He grabbed the bags of food off the passenger seat and went up the snow-covered walkway, thinking he was going to give Patrick hell for not shoveling it.

He was standing on the front porch, about to knock, when he heard a woman's laughter coming from inside. Funny, he hadn't even considered that Patrick might have female company on a Monday night. What Chase should have done was turn around and leave, but his curiosity got the best of him. The living room window was to his right, and the curtains were open, which was where the light shone from. He doubted Patrick would have left them open if there was something private going on inside. Since Patrick hadn't mentioned dating anyone, Chase deduced that one of his sisters had stopped by. But just to be sure, he decided to do some more investigation.

Wearing his expensive designer suit, wool jacket, and high-dollar leather dress shoes, Chase stepped off the porch to peer through the front window. The living room was empty even though a football game was showing on TV. Beyond the living room, he could see into the dining room, and there was the sight that would forever be etched in his brain. Patrick was standing with his back to the window, butt naked and having sex with some woman whose creamy thighs were wrapped around his waist.

Did Chase walk away then? No! Like a dirty voyeur, he stayed there for another minute, not because he'd wanted to, but because of the woman's toes. Her toenails were painted bright pink with glittery flecks on them, just like...

Holy hell! It was her. Cassandra was sprawled out on Patrick's dining room table for all the world to see. Technically, he was the only one watching, but anybody who wandered by could have seen the same thing. Never mind that it was cold and dark and nobody seemed to be outside except him.

Then, as if he'd needed the confirmation, Cassandra sat up and looked over Patrick's shoulder right at Chase. A flash of panic crossed her face, and then Patrick turned and spotted him too. Not wanting to confront them naked, Chase shot up his middle finger instead. Then he dumped the bag of Chinese food on Patrick's front porch and hurried back to his car.

By the time he'd started it and was backing out, Cassandra, wearing Patrick's robe, had opened the front door and mouthed, "I'm sorry." Ignoring her, he sped away, fueled with anger and adrenaline. Given the way he felt, it was a good thing he hadn't stayed to confront them. Who knew what he might have done to Patrick, and he couldn't afford to jeopardize his reputation and career.

Cass didn't come home that night, though she'd sent numerous texts and left voicemails apologizing. In the end, Chase sent one reply.

I'll have your stuff sent to your apartment. Don't bother coming back here.

They hadn't officially moved in together, but she'd been spending a lot of time at his place and had brought over quite a lot of stuff.

Instead of doing something destructive, like punching holes in his walls or drinking himself into oblivion, Chase took the more constructive route. He spent the next two hours shoving her things into bags and boxes without care. There wasn't much of value, but she didn't deserve for him to neatly fold her clothes. Who cared if she had to iron everything once she unpacked? It served her right!

Afterward, he slumped down on his recliner with a beer, deciding he deserved at least one for the shitty night he'd had. Sometime around one o'clock in the morning, when his eyes were mere slits, he toed off his shoes and socks and made a decision.

It was time to take a sabbatical. He'd been thinking about it recently anyway, but what he'd witnessed that night cinched it. Edwards, Stewart, and Wineman would have to do without him for a while.

His career afforded him certain luxuries, and yes, he had it made working for his dad, but being a divorce attorney wasn't all fun and games. The parade of clients with their endless bickering, name-calling, and finger-pointing wore on him. In the beginning, he'd been empathetic, at least with some. But after seeing Cass and Patrick together, he wasn't sure he could remain neutral. Cheating was one of the primary causes of divorce, and now he'd experienced it firsthand. Even though he and Cass weren't married, it still hurt like hell, and he was still consumed with anger.

His mind was made up, and the next day, he broke the news. He was taking a much-needed sabbatical somewhere far away and warm. Someplace he could recharge and reassess his life's goals and ambitions. Somewhere he could forget, at least for a while, and, hopefully, regain his optimism.

Hawaii sounded like the perfect place.

Chapter 3

One of the first things Callie noticed when she arrived at the condo was the hibiscus planted right outside the door. Flowers bloomed everywhere, and the colors made her happy, especially since all she'd been seeing for months was white snow and brown trees. Kauai was called "the Garden Island" for good reason, and she was instantly glad to be there.

She entered the code on the keypad and stepped inside, rolling one of her suitcases behind her. She'd packed a few bags since she'd be gone so long, but she'd probably overdone it, since Hawaii was one of the most laid-back places on earth. An assortment of shorts, T-shirts, bathing suits, and sundresses was all she needed, but she'd also had to bring her writing paraphernalia, including journals, reference books, pens, notepads, and of course, her laptop.

Up until recently, her laptop had been her most prized possession, but right then, she didn't even want to think about it. She planned to take the next few days to get acclimated and enjoy the sights, and then she'd think about writing.

She felt wistful as she rolled the suitcase into the bedroom, which had an ocean view. It was the same unit she'd stayed at several years ago, but the décor had changed. Still, it brought back a slew of memories as she walked through the rooms and refamiliarized herself with the layout.

Once she'd brought in all the bags and stowed them away, she decided to step outside and get some air. After being cooped up in an airplane and then a car, she was anxious to stretch her legs. It was early afternoon, and the outdoor thermometer next to the patio door read seventy-two degrees. The sun was bright, there was a slight breeze, and the ocean dazzled where it met the shore.

Her grandma had been right. Hawaii was one of the most romantic places on earth and should be the ideal location to write once she was ready. But for now, she decided to take the resort path down to the beach.

She was still wearing her travel clothes, as she hadn't wanted to take the time to change. Besides, it wasn't so hot that yoga pants, an oversized T-shirt, and sneakers looked out of place. Later, she'd unpack and change into something more resort-like.

She loved the tranquility of Kauai. Rather than city sounds, she heard birds chirping, children laughing as they splashed in the pool, and the wind rustling in the palm trees. The only thing missing was having someone to enjoy it with. She'd promised herself not to get melancholy, though. This was meant to be a trip that rejuvenated her, not a reminder of all she'd lost.

She paused where the cement path ended at the beach, which was small and C-shaped. The water looked innocent enough, but she recalled the strong undercurrent and how she'd felt more comfortable swimming in the pool. There were several people laying out but only two brave young men were in the water, dressed in full bodysuits and trying to surf. She watched them for a while and admired their tenacity before turning around to head back.

When she got closer to her unit, she could see the pool, and something caught her attention, or more accurately, someone. A man was pacing the pool deck with a phone pressed to his ear. He looked disgruntled, his mouth set in a tight line and his posture tense. Scanning his body, she noted his muscular chest and toned arms and legs. He was wearing black swim trunks, sunglasses, and nothing else.

She glanced around to see if anybody had noticed her staring, but she was alone. Since she couldn't keep standing there, she very slowly continued up the path toward her unit while keeping the man in sight.

Suddenly he stopped pacing and shoved his left hand in his wavy brown hair. As a writer, she paid close attention to details, and she noticed he wasn't wearing a ring. But that didn't mean he was unattached.

If Quinn were there, she'd have been drooling and dragging them to the pool to get acquainted. But Callie wasn't here for that and was content to admire him from afar. It had been a while since she'd noticed a man like him. But here, without any distractions, he stood out like the colorful hibiscus growing by her front door.

When he resumed pacing, she allowed her eyes to roam over his backside, which was high and round, completing his perfect body. A man who looked like that could only mean one thing—trouble with a capital T! However, he had the exact physical type of a romance book hero.

She didn't even need to know his personality to use him as a character. She could make it up. *Hmm.* Would he be cocky, arrogant, and controlling? Did he have a tortured soul? A troubled childhood? A string of failed relationships? Had he just lost someone he loved—a parent, spouse, friend, or lover? The possibilities were endless, which was why she enjoyed writing so much.

She could concoct a story about a complete stranger, and she had full creative license. The guy would never even have to know.

This could be his last day on the island, and she might never see him again, but she'd already imprinted his image on her brain, and she could easily recall it when she sat down to write. At least, it used to be that easy.

Sighing, she tore her eyes away and picked up her pace. She'd been standing and gawking long enough, and she didn't want to get caught.

If, by chance, she saw him around there again, he was fair game, though. In addition to her attention to detail, she excelled at blending into the background. She could observe him unnoticed since there was nothing about her that stood out.

If Irene or Quinn were there, they'd have argued with her, but she wasn't being self-critical, just honest. She had straight dark brown hair styled in a mid-length bob and matching brown eyes. When she wrote, she wore black-framed glasses, but typically she went without. She had some freckles (more like tiny moles) across her nose and cheeks that she used to try and cover up, but now she let them be. Quinn said they reminded her of Meghan Markle. Ha! She wished!

Chasing Forever

Her body was in decent shape, though it was nowhere near as fit as Superman's over there. Walking and bike-riding were her favorite physical activities, and ice-skating helped keep the winter pounds to a minimum, but she wasn't one to pass up dessert or ban certain foods altogether. Life was too short for that, and she enjoyed her three squares.

Average and normal (most of the time) were words she'd use to describe herself. Nothing to sneeze at yet nothing to get excited about either. She was ensconced somewhere in the middle, which was not the position one wanted to be in to snag a guy like him.

Therefore, she'd be content to sit back and observe while taking copious amounts of notes that would miraculously result in an irresistible romantic hero. It was like performing a magic trick with the opportunity to do it over if it didn't turn out right the first time. The magic of computers!

She took one last glance at Mr. Hottie and noticed he'd sat down on the lounge chair with his hands behind his head, looking much more relaxed than he had a few minutes ago. With his sunglasses on, it was difficult to tell where he was looking and if his eyes were even open. But she didn't want to risk him spotting her, so she quickly crossed the lawn and let herself back into the safety of her condo.

After changing into shorts and a T-shirt that read "Vacay Mode," she took a notepad and pen out of her messenger bag, poured herself a tall glass of ice water, and stepped out onto the patio. From there, she had a limited view of the pool, which was fine. She simply wanted to jot down a few ideas before she forgot them.

She traded her shades for her regular glasses and bent over her hardbound notebook. After being a writer for several years, it still amazed her how the brain and pen worked in tandem, and soon she had a whole page of notes. Some of them were snippets of details, like hair color, eye color, height, skin tone, etc. Others were random ideas for the character's backstory.

She might end up using all, some, or none of them, but at least she had a start. She was still deep in thought, pen poised at her mouth, when a movement caught her eye. She glanced up and about fell off her chair.

Mr. Hottie, aka potential romance book hero, was walking toward her, shirtless and with a towel draped casually over one arm. His hair was wet and slicked back, and water droplets clung to his bare chest with its perfect smattering of hair.

Why isn't he walking on the path? Where is he going? Why does it look like he's headed straight for me? She pretended to stare at her notebook while simultaneously tracking his every step. It was quite the feat, and with her eyes cast downward, she saw his feet. Naturally, they were as perfect as the rest of him.

She expected him to stop or change course at any second, but he just kept coming until he paused at the half wall separating her patio from the next-door neighbor's. *Keep your eyes down. He probably won't even notice me.*

"Oh. Hey. Almost didn't see you there."

Wait a minute. Is he talking to me? Is he talking to me? Stop with the movie quotes!

Raising her head like she'd just seen him for the first time, she said, "Hello." It was all she could manage because, at close range, he was even more beautiful than from a distance. She wanted him to say whatever it was he had to say and move on so she could pick her tongue up off the ground and continue writing.

"Looks like we're neighbors," he said with a smile.

"Oh, yeah?" She adopted an air of nonchalance, though she was feeling anything but. This could not be happening unless she'd accidentally stepped into the pages of one of her romance books and was acting out a scene.

"Just get here?"

"Um-hmm. You?"

"Yep. Earlier today."

So far, their conversation was much less impressive than his looks, but that was partially her fault. She always wrote better than she spoke, but she was particularly tongue-tied with him standing so close and dripping water onto her patio floor.

"Me too."

"I'm Chase Edwards, by the way."

Of course you are. You had to have a romance hero's name to match your looks!

"Callie Cooper. Nice to meet you."

He came closer, his arm outstretched to shake her hand, and the blood started pounding in her ears. Forcing an outward calm, she closed her notebook, set down her pen, and reciprocated. They shook hands across the table, a drop of water from his chest plopping onto the cover of her notebook and spreading.

"Sorry about that. I just got out of the pool." He leaned over and dried the spot with his towel, which gave her an even closer look at his face. This right here was how romance novels were born.

Adam used to chide her that no human being looked as good as a character in one of her books. *Guess what, buddy? You were wrong like you were about so many other things...*

Just then, her phone rang on the table, and Quinn's name appeared on the screen.

Chase seemed relieved by the interruption and quickly stepped back. "Go ahead and take it. I'll see you around."

She gave him a brief wave, picked up her phone, and hurried inside. Wait until Quinn heard about this!

Chapter 4

Damn! They were everywhere. It was going to be next to impossible to keep himself to himself on this trip. He'd already met two women at the pool—friends who were there for a week on a "girls' trip." Kelsey and Tina were a little young for him, but hey, he was on vacation!

Then there was the hot woman next door—Callie. At first glance, she'd reminded him of a sexy professor he'd once had, or maybe it was the librarian. In any case, he was a sucker for an attractive woman wearing glasses. And yes, he'd always imagined the glasses being whipped off in the heat of passion, or in Callie's case, she'd probably carefully set them aside.

That was his impression of her—pretty without really owning it and maybe a bit uptight. Or maybe she was just smart and careful. She'd seemed reserved when he'd introduced himself, but who could blame her? She had no idea who he was or what he was after. She'd played it cool, and that was a smart move.

On the other hand, Kelsey and Tina had acted exactly the opposite. They'd eyed him like a piece of candy, which he hadn't minded, before they'd come over and introduced themselves. They'd exchanged names and pleasantries before sashaying back to their lounge chairs on the opposite side of the pool.

He considered himself an intelligent person, and even though he'd been blindsided by Cassandra, he still trusted his instincts. He had a hunch that should he want to pursue either of the women (or maybe even both), they wouldn't turn him down. They'd been giddy, flirtatious, and quite possibly intoxicated, but he hadn't really been interested, and that bugged the crap out of him.

Since when did he turn down a sure thing? What healthy single male wouldn't want to pursue two sexy females who seemed receptive?

He would have liked to blame it all on Cass, but the truth was he'd turned sour and cynical because of his job. His clients were people who'd professed to love and cherish their spouses until death, yet while they were in his office, you'd never know it.

After everything he'd seen and heard, he couldn't help but become hardened. He knew of very few success stories, his own parents being one of the exceptions. His dad, Daniel, and Daniel's two partners owned Edwards, Stewart, and Wineman, and it had seemed inevitable that Chase would join them someday.

From a young age, he'd helped with menial tasks around the office, but he'd also picked up the jargon, become familiar with legal documents, and gained invaluable insight into the profession.

After law school, he'd immediately joined his dad's firm. He'd had to prove himself just like anyone else, but he was a quick study and a hard worker, and the law came easy to him.

It wasn't until recently that he'd started feeling a niggle of dissatisfaction and started questioning his career choice. He still wanted to practice law, but he was considering moving into a different niche such as estate planning, where the aim was to provide for one's family, not tear it apart.

But he didn't have to decide immediately. He had the next eight weeks to mull it over. In the meantime, he planned on doing all the things tourists do in Hawaii: sunbathe, swim, snorkel, hike, eat pineapple, and relax.

He'd try to avoid: buying a flowery Hawaiian shirt, eating *too much* pineapple, getting sunburned, and getting involved with a woman (or two, as the case might be).

Anyway, what was the point unless he just wanted to get laid? After eight weeks, he'd be leaving, and he'd never see the woman again.

Wait a minute, you idiot! That's exactly the point. A no-strings, harmless, fun-in-the-sun affair. *What's wrong with me? Has the sun already fried my brain?* That did it. Tomorrow he'd seek out Kelsey and Tina. But tonight he was too exhausted.

He decided to get dressed, drive to the nearest town for dinner, and hit the hay early. A good meal and a solid night's rest would revive him, and maybe tomorrow he'd start to get his mojo back.

Mojo? Now, that's a word I haven't used in a long time...

Chapter 5

After consulting her Kauai travel guide, Callie settled on Puka Dog for dinner. Quinn would probably tease her for choosing a hot dog joint out of all the options, but it was quick, convenient, and according to the travel guide, the best hot dog place on the island. Besides, she was too tired to sit down to a full-course meal. She just wanted to eat and then return to the condo and go to sleep. She had eight weeks to try other restaurants.

She pulled into the shopping center where the restaurant was located and parked. It was dusk now, but the air was still warm, and she liked that she didn't have to bundle up like she'd been doing at home.

Puka Dog was easy to find, and soon she was standing in line behind several other people waiting to order. Seeing how busy it was assured her she'd made the right choice.

"Next!" shouted a young guy who was taking orders.

When the next person stepped up to the counter, Callie sucked in a breath. *No. It can't be him. Out of all the restaurants on the island, he wouldn't have picked this one. But wait a minute, I did!*

Even though his back was to her, she recognized that body and his voice. This was one of the few times she didn't mind being short, or petite, as Quinn called her. She could successfully hide behind the tall guy in front of her and observe Chase without him knowing.

She listened while he placed his order and then stepped up to the register to pay. She watched closely as he handed the pretty cashier his American Express card, and she saw the girl's cheeks flush as she rang up his order.

Of course. Any woman, young, old, or in between, would have to be blind not to notice him. This was another reason why he'd make the perfect romance hero.

Making sure to stay behind the beanpole in front of her, she waited to see where Chase would sit. The restaurant offered indoor and outdoor seating, and she placed her bet on the latter. She'd wanted to sit outside too, but she didn't want him to see her.

She wasn't interested in making friends with him. She simply wanted to observe and use him as her muse. She also didn't want him to think she was following him, because she wasn't. How could she know he liked hot dogs as much as she did? Honestly, he didn't even look like a hot dog kind of guy. Sushi maybe...

"Next!"

Beanpole suddenly stepped aside and said, "You can go ahead. I'm waiting for my girlfriend."

Callie panicked. She'd wanted to hide behind him until Chase sat down. Peering out of the corner of her eye, she saw Chase's back as he went outside with his food tray.

She sighed with relief and proceeded to place her order.

Once she had her food, she peeked out the front window to get the lay of the land. Was this what private investigators felt like? Lurking around in order to see and not be seen? Good thing she was a writer instead, because she'd be terrible at it!

She didn't spot him at any of the nearby tables, so she decided to take a chance. Tipping her head down, she carefully stepped outside with her food tray and made a beeline for the first available table.

Good move. Chase was sitting a few tables away with his back to her. He had his phone out and was scrolling through it in between bites of hot dog.

Chasing Forever

She settled in and placed her phone on the table, but she didn't plan on looking at it. She was much more interested in what he was doing.

When she took her first bite of hot dog topped with pineapple relish, though, she forgot all about her mission. The travel writer had been spot-on. This was by far the best hot dog she'd ever tasted.

For the next few minutes, she enjoyed the food and surroundings while observing Chase at the same time. He'd stopped scrolling through his phone and was sipping a lemonade while glancing at the passersby.

Soon she realized how silly this was. The man wasn't doing anything worthy of a romantic hero. He was simply relaxing like she was, though he still looked the part.

Tonight, he was wearing khaki shorts, a striped polo shirt, and canvas slip-on shoes. He could have been any other man on vacation, and it was dark, so hardly anybody noticed him.

Maybe she'd been wrong about him. Maybe he'd wanted to blend in and not "be seen." Hmm. She was still contemplating this when he suddenly moved his seat back and started to stand up.

Shit, shit, shit! She quickly picked up her phone and bent over it so her hair was partially blocking her face. He surely wouldn't recognize her now, plus she wasn't wearing her glasses this time.

Keeping her head down, she could still sense his movements, and as he came closer with his tray, she prayed he wouldn't notice her. She saw the briefest glimpse of khaki pass in and out of her peripheral vision and thought she was in the clear, but then the khakis reappeared right at the edge of her table.

"Callie? Is that you?"

She popped her head up and feigned surprise. "Oh, hi. Chase, right?" *As if I'd forget his name!*

"Right. What a surprise to see you here."

She could have said the same of him. "I know, right? Out of all the restaurants on the island!"

He smiled, and his teeth glistened like in a toothpaste commercial. "I guess we're both fans of hot dogs."

"Yep. The all-American food!" *Do I sound as dorky to him as I do to myself? God, I hope not.*

"True, but with a Hawaiian flare. It was delicious."

"I agree."

"Well, I'll let you get back to it," he said, motioning to her phone.

Luckily, the screen had gone dark. She'd been looking at her own books on Amazon to read the latest customer reviews, but he didn't need to know what she did for a living. She was just some woman who happened to be staying at the same resort as him, and she wanted to keep it that way.

Chasing Forever

"Okay. Have a nice night."
"You too."

She'd often been asked how she came up with the material for her books. While it would have been nice to have a clever answer, there was none. Most of her ideas popped into her head at unexpected times and places, and often in the middle of the night. Sometimes she'd jolt awake at two or three in the morning with an idea that she'd be compelled to write down. When she and Adam had first started living together, he'd found it disruptive, but eventually he'd gotten used to it. It had become such a common occurrence that she always kept notepads and pens on her bedside table—until recently.

That night, she'd been sleeping soundly when suddenly she sat upright. An idea had presented itself, startling her since it hadn't happened in so long. It took her a moment to get her bearings. Glancing at the clock on the bedside table, she saw it was three thirty in the morning, and she remembered she was in Hawaii.

Then she reached over for a notepad and pen and realized she hadn't placed any there. Torn between feeling irritated and invigorated, she shoved off the covers and climbed out of bed. She immediately reached for her robe, though she didn't even need it.

It was still warm out, unlike at home, where the temperatures would be hovering in the teens. Padding out of the bedroom, she went into the living room, where she'd left all her writing supplies. She'd planned to grab a notepad and pen and go right back to the bedroom, but then she heard a strange noise coming from next door. *Is Chase awake too?*

She stilled for a moment, thinking she might have imagined it, but then she heard it again. Tiptoeing across the living room, she went into the kitchen, which abutted his unit. She quietly took out a glass from the cupboard, put the opening to the wall, and pressed her ear against the bottom of it. She heard music and Chase's voice as he sang along.

Seriously? He was listening to rock and roll and singing at three thirty in the morning? Didn't he realize some people were trying to sleep? (Or at least they were supposed to be.)

Since she'd gone this far, she listened a while longer until she identified the song. It was Whitesnake singing "Here I Go Again," and she only knew that because Quinn was a fan of eighties rock.

Her mind immediately started whirring. Why had he chosen that song? It had a lonely, melancholy vibe to it. Was that how Chase felt? What was his reason for being here, and why wasn't he asleep? Setting the glass down, she decided to mull it over in bed, though she liked listening to him. His voice was deep and soothing, if not completely on key.

Then she imagined his deep, soothing voice whispering in her ear, or in her book heroine's ear, and she shivered. That did it! She needed to write down her ideas, and tomorrow morning she'd attempt to write an outline or maybe even the first chapter.

It almost felt like he'd been singing the song to her, but instead of interpreting it as a lonely lament, she found it inspiring. "Here *I* go again. My writer's juices are flowing. Thanks, Chase," she whispered and padded back to bed.

Chapter 6

The next morning, Chase slept in since he'd been up half the night. It would take a while to adjust to Hawaii time, but that was a minor sacrifice. His sister, Miranda, had texted him a selfie of her scraping the ice off her windshield that morning, so he had nothing to complain about. Besides, this was the day he was going to try to get his mojo back.

He dug through his suitcase for a different pair of swim trunks than he'd worn the day before. It wasn't a matter of fashion but necessity since he'd forgotten to hang up his black ones and they were lying in a damp pile on the bathroom floor.

"Just because you're on vacation, it doesn't mean you have to be a slob," he admonished himself as he draped the trunks over the shower door to dry.

Chasing Forever

He hung around the condo until early afternoon, when he figured there'd be a good chance of running into Kelsey and Tina at the pool.

He slipped on his shades and slides, slung a towel over his arm, grabbed his book (a new thriller he'd been dying to read), and stepped outside. Instead of rushing to the pool, he paused for a moment and just breathed. The air was warm but not hot, and the ocean spread out before him, dazzling in the sun. Hawaii was showing off again, and he was about to do the same.

But before he stepped off the patio, he heard a familiar sound coming from next door. Thinking he might have imagined it, he stayed very still and listened, a smile spreading across his face.

Callie likes Whitesnake too? She was listening to "Here I Go Again," the same song he'd been listening to last night when he couldn't sleep. *Bizarre!* He'd never have pegged her as someone who'd like rock music. She seemed more like an Ed Sheeran or Michael Bublé fan—something softer and sweeter.

He shook his head as he walked away, thinking, *You never really know people until you actually know them, and even then, they surprise you.* An image of Cass and Patrick came to mind, and he bristled. *Dammit!* He thought he'd be over it by now, but bad memories had a way of sneaking up on you.

"Shake it off," he mumbled as he approached the pool gate.

Letting himself in, he glanced around and realized he practically had the place to himself. There was a young family of four in the pool and an older woman reading on one of the lounge chairs, but no sign of Kelsey and Tina.

He hated to admit it, but he didn't really mind. He'd be perfectly content reading until they showed up, and even if they didn't, he'd still be okay. There were plenty of things to do in Hawaii besides chasing women in bikinis, though he'd never tell his buddies that. He'd let them think he was getting some action on vacation, even if it only amounted to the self-provided kind.

He took a chair with an unobstructed view of the pool gate and settled in. Twenty minutes later, he was immersed in his novel when he heard a woman giggling, and he glanced up to see Kelsey and Tina entering the pool area.

Scanning the pool deck, their eyes landed on him, and they smiled and waved. They were both hot in an obvious, showy sort of way, especially Kelsey, with her long chestnut brown hair, curvy body, and seductive smile. Tina reminded him a little too much of Cass, with her blonde hair, blue eyes, and light skin, but he wasn't supposed to be thinking about Cass right now.

"Good afternoon, ladies," he said as they approached.

"Hi!" Kelsey said, and Tina just smiled and nodded.

"Care to join me?"

"We'd love to!"

Obviously, Kelsey was the spokesperson for the team, and Tina seemed to go along with whatever she said. Not that it really mattered, but he preferred a woman with a little more backbone.

They took chairs on either side of him and laid out their towels. They were both wearing cover-ups, though the term was misleading. Kelsey's was of the mesh variety, and he could see her bright yellow bikini through the material. He also spotted a small butterfly tattoo on her right hip and stared at it for a moment.

He wasn't really a fan of ink, especially on women. A woman's body was so naturally beautiful that he hated to see it marred, particularly when it had been done on purpose. Thinking of a woman's body, with its soft, smooth skin, reminded him that he hadn't touched one in a while. If he got the opportunity, he hoped he'd remember what to do. *You idiot! It hasn't been that long!*

Tina's cover-up looked like an oversized T-shirt that she slipped over her head with ease, like it didn't bother her at all to undress in public. Today she was wearing a blue bikini with a top that resembled a push-up bra. He hadn't noticed her breasts the other day, but now they were spilling over the top. Had she worn it for his benefit? He doubted it. These women were on vacation, and they obviously had an agenda. If not him, it would be some other guy. If his friend Eric were there, he'd probably call Chase a "lucky bastard."

It took them a while to get settled, and when Tina bent over to rummage through her beach bag, he got an even better look at her breasts. Whoever said, "Men are visual creatures," was right. Even if these two women weren't the cream of the crop, they were there and almost naked, and they wanted to sit with him (or maybe even on him). He couldn't help it. He simply had to look.

Tina stood up with her sunscreen in hand, and then another movement caught his attention. *Callie*.

At least, he thought it was her. She was wearing a big floppy hat, sunglasses, and a black cover-up with a zipper. Now there was an actual cover-up. He couldn't see anything underneath, which he found enticing. He liked that she'd left something to the imagination, unlike the two bathing beauties beside him.

"Chase? Would you mind rubbing some lotion on my back?" Kelsey's voice snapped him out of his reverie.

"Oh. Sure," he said, taking the bottle of sunscreen from her.

She perched on the edge of her chair, facing away from him, and swung her silky brown hair to one side, giving him access to her back. It also allowed him to keep an eye on Callie, and he watched her decide where to sit.

There appeared to be a method to it. First, she glanced skyward to assess the position of the sun. Next, she viewed the available chairs in relation to it. If she'd spotted him before, she hadn't given any indication, but as her eyes traveled around the pool deck, they alighted on him, and she paused.

He could practically see the wheels spinning in her head. *Do I acknowledge him even though he's occupied, or do I ignore the horny bastard flanked by two equally horny bikini-clad women?*

She settled for a brief nod and then turned her back on him to select her chair. She'd chosen one at a diagonal to his instead of directly across, and he thought he understood why. She didn't seem to be the nosy type, and if she were curious about what was going on with the three of them, she wouldn't show it. Callie was too mature for that. He wasn't sure why she was in Hawaii, but she seemed to have a very different agenda than the two women sitting beside him.

"Mmm. That feels so good," Kelsey said as he massaged the lotion into her skin.

He'd been so caught up watching Callie that he'd almost forgotten what he was doing.

"It's my turn now," Tina said, with a huff.

Maybe Tina wasn't such a pushover after all. She rose up a notch in his mind, though he was still distracted by the petite brunette across the pool.

Taking the bottle of sunscreen from Tina, he poured some in his hand but then paused.

Callie was standing beside her chair with her back to him, but he could tell she was unzipping her cover-up. This he had to see.

"Chase?" Tina said with an annoying whine in her voice.

"Oh. Right. Sorry."

She tipped her head down, and he started spreading the lotion across her upper back.

"Don't forget under the straps," she said.

If she thought she'd sounded seductive, she'd been wrong. It was more like a princess giving an order to a servant. Still, doing this gave him an excuse to observe Callie without anyone knowing it.

Callie was now shrugging off her cover-up and slowly revealing one inch of skin at a time. First, her neck and shoulders appeared, and he saw a simple black tie around her neck. He was familiar with the terminology of women's clothing having grown up with a sister, and he guessed it was a halter-style top. Interesting choice. If for some reason that tie came undone...

"Lower, please," Tina demanded.

Chase poured more sunscreen into his palm and realized it was sweaty even though it wasn't that hot out. As he rubbed the lotion in circular motions on Tina's lower back, Callie peeled the cover-up down her arms, and with a quick swoop, it was off.

Chase sucked in a breath. She was wearing a plain black one-piece—ultra conservative to most but sexy as hell to him. He saw enough of her skin to notice its smooth, even texture, and it made him want to see more.

As if she'd read his mind, Callie laid the cover-up at the end of her chair and faced forward, allowing him to see the front view and proving why he found one-piece swimsuits sexy. The material clung to her curves while still leaving a lot to the imagination. The halter top dipped low enough to show a hint of cleavage but not low enough to be obscene. The legs of the swimsuit were cut higher to elongate her legs, and he guessed she'd chosen it because of her small stature.

She was petite, another characteristic he found appealing in women. Something about it called out to the Neanderthal in him, making him feel like the big, strong male who'd been designed to protect and defend. The idea was antiquated and probably offensive to some, but hey, he was just being honest.

She slipped off her flip-flops and sat down, her floppy hat and sunglasses concealing much of her face and making her appear sun-savvy and sexy.

"I think that's good," Tina said, wincing.

Judging by her tone, he'd been rubbing in the lotion with a bit too much force.

They sat back in their chairs, and he glanced over at Kelsey, who was scrolling through her phone.

Was this how it was going to be? If they didn't want to engage in conversation, how were they supposed to get to know each other? But Kelsey and Tina seemed perfectly content to just lie there like he was a decoration or something.

He heard Eric's voice in his head, yelling, "So what! Enjoy it! You'll probably get laid tonight."

He leaned back and crossed his arms behind his head, adopting a casual pose like he was used to being flanked by two bikini-clad women he didn't even know. His eyes, though, stayed trained on Callie. Thank God she couldn't see him behind his sunglasses.

What's she doing now? *Hmm*. She pulled out a notepad and pen like she had the other day. Was she a reporter or something? Was she obsessed with journaling? Was she recording her vacation memories for posterity's sake?

Why is this so fascinating to me? Why is she here? She didn't seem like the type to travel alone. He'd noticed she didn't wear a ring, but maybe her boyfriend was meeting her here. Maybe he was going to show up any minute. Now who was the lucky bastard?

Chapter 7

Chase and *two* women? That was NOT a romance novel she wanted to write! He was messing up her plot. Couldn't he have been satisfied with just one?

Those were Callie's thoughts when she first spotted Chase sitting between two young, attractive women in brightly colored bikinis. First, she was glad he was there, thinking he might spark some more material for her book. But she became irritated when she saw him rubbing suntan lotion on the brunette *and* the blonde.

Seriously? This stuff happened in real life? She'd always known it, but somehow it seemed more feasible in fiction. How did it work? Did they take turns? And perhaps the most pressing question of all, why would anyone want to share? She couldn't imagine that. Well, she could, but she didn't want to.

Chase was wearing sunglasses, so she couldn't see his eyes, but she swore he was looking at her instead of what he was doing. While his hands moved on the brunette's back, his head was angled in her direction. Rather than feeling flattered, she felt disconcerted. Why would he be looking at her when he had two half-naked women at his fingertips—literally? It didn't make any sense.

Plus, she was wearing her "matronly" swimsuit (according to Quinn) that was designed for function over fashion. She liked that she could actually swim in it without anything coming loose and sliding up or down. It was practical, and since she wasn't out to impress anyone, she'd been fine with it. She was dumbfounded that Chase would be looking at her instead of the eye candy on either side of him.

But since she was there, she might as well use the opportunity to take a few more notes. She'd spent the morning drafting an outline based on her middle-of-the-night epiphany, but she hadn't written the first chapter yet. She'd decided to set her romance in Hawaii because, hello, it was the perfect location. The story would be about two strangers who met and eventually fell in love. The conflict was inherent. What would happen when the vacation ended and the characters had to return to their regular lives? To make it even more problematic, what if one of them lived on the East Coast and the other on the West? The possibilities were endless, and she'd still been fleshing it out when she'd realized it was mid-afternoon, and she'd wanted to take a swim.

She hadn't even considered that Chase might be at the pool with *two* women, but maybe it was meant to be. If she kept running into him, she'd have plenty of fodder for her character. Not knowing Chase wasn't a problem because she could assign him whatever traits she wanted to, though she hadn't planned on making him polyamorous!

Leaning over, she took a pen and notepad out of her beach bag. But while she was thinking about what to write, she glanced across the pool and caught eyes with him. He smiled and gave her a brief wave. There was no doubt it was meant for her because the only other person on her side of the pool was an elderly lady sprawled out napping and snoring.

Not wanting to be rude, she gave him a brief wave in return, but then she averted her gaze to the notebook. The Barbies had to be dumb (no offense — she'd loved Barbies as a child), to be sitting next to him and not notice that he was flirting with someone else.

But the brunette seemed enthralled with something on her phone, and the blonde might have been sleeping. She was lying so still that the only evidence she was alive was the slight rise and fall of her bountiful breasts as she breathed.

Callie suppressed the urge to yell, "Boobs, Chase. Boobs! Right next to you. Why are you looking at me?"

After a few more minutes of pretending to concentrate on her work, she put the notepad aside in frustration. There were too many distractions between the snoring granny to her right and the confusing man across the pool, so she gave up.

Since she was in her swimsuit and the pool was gloriously empty now that the family of four had left, she decided to take a dip. After all, that's what she'd come there for.

She stood up and removed her hat and sunglasses, carefully placing them in her tote and sliding it under the chair. Then she walked past snoring granny and over to the steps that led into the shallow end of the pool.

She dipped a toe in the water to test the temperature, and finding it cool but not cold, she decided to venture in. She slowly immersed herself, descending one step at a time and trying hard not to look in Chase's direction.

At the shallowest point, the water barely came up to her knees, but a few more steps and she'd be at the four feet mark. After that, it plunged to six feet, which would be way over her head. Her choices were to splash around in the shallow end like a kid or dive under and swim like an adult. She chose the latter, pointing her hands out in front like an arrow and diving under.

After the initial shock to her system, she loosened up and swam underwater to the deep end. Then she popped up, turned around, and swam back to where she'd started.

This time, when she popped her head out of the water, Chase was sitting on one of the steps and smiling. "Hey," he said as she wiped the water out of her eyes.

"Hey."

"You made it look too tempting."

"Tempting?" She tilted her head, thinking she might still have water in her ears.

He chuckled, the sound deep and soothing like his voice when he'd been singing last night. "The water. You made it look inviting."

Is he flirting with me? Because this is NOT necessary for me to write my book. "Well, we are at the pool, so it makes sense that someone should swim in it."

He nodded and eyed her quizzically.

She realized she hadn't been overly friendly toward him and maybe she should loosen up a little. If they talked more, it might help her story. But she wondered if he was capable of having a normal conversation without flirting.

"I see you're here with some friends," she said, motioning over her shoulder.

He tipped his head down and rubbed the back of his neck, almost like he was ashamed. Ashamed? Not her romantic hero. He was a pro with the ladies—smooth, laid-back, confident.

"Yeah, well, I wouldn't exactly call them friends."

"Oh?"

"I just met them. What about you? Are you here with anyone?"

"Why do you ask?" She'd wanted to let her guard down, but it was difficult. If he was a player, she didn't want to play, and she wanted to make that clear.

"Just curious."

He must have misread her disgruntled expression because he hurriedly added, "Don't worry. I'm not a serial killer or anything. Just making conversation."

"I'm here alone," she confirmed after a beat. He might be a player, but she didn't believe he meant any harm.

"Ah."

"But my best friend might come and visit sometime during my stay."

"How long will you be here?"

"A while. You?"

"Eight weeks."

"Wow. I guess you'll have time to make a lot of *friends*, then."

He tipped his head back and laughed, and she laughed too, though she felt somewhat embarrassed. She hadn't wanted him to think she was paying that close attention to him. If she were a detective, she'd fire herself.

"I didn't really come here to make friends," he said, his smile receding. "I actually came here to be alone."

"Me too."

"Yeah?"

She nodded. "It's been a rough year…" She hadn't meant to go there, but it was too late.

Chase studied her closely. "I can relate." He looked like he was about to say more, but then his gaze shifted to the right, and she followed its path.

Blonde Barbie had finally woken up and was walking toward them. "How's the water? Is it cold?"

Callie watched her sidle up next to Chase and place a hand on his shoulder in a possessive gesture. She pointed her toes like a ballerina and skimmed the surface of the water to test it. So far, she hadn't acknowledged Callie's presence at all, which wasn't surprising.

She must have looked like a drowned rat compared to blondie, and she ran her hands over her hair self-consciously. She hadn't budged since she and Chase had started talking, but now she decided to get out of the pool.

Ignoring blondie, Chase said, "Done swimming already?"

Callie nodded. "I just wanted to cool off."

Blondie ran her hand down Chase's arm and grabbed his hand, tugging on it like a child. "Come in with me," she mewled.

Chase shot Callie an apologetic look and then allowed blondie to drag him forward into the pool. As they passed, his eyes roamed over Callie's wet body, and glancing down, she realized why. Crossing her arms over her chest, she got out of the pool and hurried across the cement to her chair.

While her bathing suit was conservative, it hadn't hidden her pointy nipples as she'd emerged from the cool water into the warm air. *Damn you, nipples!*

She couldn't wrap the towel around herself fast enough, and then she plopped down on the chair and pretended to relax while she watched the rest of the show.

Chase was leaning against the opposite side of the pool now with his arms spread out along the ledge. At first, Callie thought he was holding himself up, but then she realized he was standing in the six-foot section. Reaching into her tote bag, she pulled out her notepad again and jotted "Over six feet tall" next to the list of her hero's attributes.

In the meantime, blondie was happily clinging to his side. It was either that or drown since she wasn't over six feet. If Callie had to guess, she'd put her at about five feet seven. Everyone was taller than her.

Trying not to be too obvious, Callie observed them in between taking notes. Chase appeared to be torn between looking at her and the wet, clinging woman at his side. Then the brunette rose from her lounge chair and walked over to join them.

This should be interesting.

Instead of getting into the pool, the brunette sat on Chase's other side and dangled her legs in. He was the meat in a bikini sandwich, but for some reason, he didn't look thrilled about it. The poor guy didn't know where to look, but Callie didn't feel sorry for him. She was more curious than anything, and a tiny bit jealous if she were being honest.

She and Chase had been close to having a real conversation before blondie had interrupted. When they'd been talking, he'd given her his full attention, and she'd liked it. He'd seemed genuinely interested in her, even if she'd looked like a drowned rat compared to the bikini models beside him.

The brunette leaned in and whispered something in Chase's ear. Whatever it was made his eyebrows raise above his sunglasses, and then the brunette laughed. Blondie, not to be outdone, whispered in his other ear, and Callie swore she saw his face turn red. Maybe the redness was from being in the sun too long, though she doubted it.

At that point, she decided she'd seen enough. She stood up, dropped her towel, and reached for her cover-up. Somehow it had fallen off the chair and was lying on the ground, forcing her to bend over to retrieve it. Once she'd put it on and was zipping it up, she glanced over at Chase, and sure enough, he was looking straight at her.

If he'd thought she'd given him a butt shot on purpose, he was dead wrong, but she smiled at the idea of it. Maybe she'd even write that into her story. She didn't look at him again until she'd gone out of the pool gate and turned around to latch it.

His girls were back by their chairs, packing up their belongings and chatting happily while Chase stood apart and dried himself off with his towel. Callie couldn't help but stare for a minute. The man was an object of beauty, which was why he made the perfect muse. But there was something else there too, something she suspected the two Barbies weren't interested in, but she was.

What made him tick? What had happened this past year that made him come here alone? And why did he seem more curious about her than his *friends*? Who was this man she'd chosen as her hero? And the most perplexing question of all—why did she care?

Chapter 8

After lounging around the resort for a few days, Chase decided it was time to get out and do something "touristy." He consulted Google and decided to go snorkeling at Poipu Beach, which was nearby on the south shore of the island.

After stopping in town to rent some equipment, he pulled into the beach parking lot, which was already filled with cars. Supposedly, it was one of the most popular beaches on the island, and aside from the excellent snorkeling, there was a good chance of spotting monk seals sunning themselves on the warm white sand.

Chase grabbed all his gear and headed out to claim his own patch of sand. He laid out a towel, sat down, removed his shirt, and stuffed it into his bag. Leaning back on his elbows with his shades on, he surveyed the scene.

Beaches were made for people-watching, and for a while, that was what he did. This was a family-friendly beach, and he smiled at the children splashing and playing at the water's edge. Farther out, heads bobbed in and out of the water, and snorkeling tubes jutted into the air. Every so often, someone would motion excitedly to the water where they must have spotted an exotic fish or interesting sea creature.

But he wasn't in a hurry to join them. He had all day and the next several weeks, and he could take his time. It was refreshing not having to answer to anyone, and he planned to take full advantage of his freedom. All too soon, he'd be back at the office, dealing with other people's problems. But for now, he was going to adopt the Hawaiian slogan "Hang loose!" Maybe he'd even break down and buy a T-shirt with the phrase on it.

He could have used that philosophy a few nights ago when Kelsey and Tina had propositioned him...

After hanging out at the pool, they suggested going for dinner and drinks at a local bar. Not seeing any harm in it, he agreed, and they drove there together—his first mistake of the evening.

At first, everything was fine. They talked over appetizers and drinks (fruity cocktails for the women and beer for him). It wasn't riveting conversation, but it was pleasant, and the atmosphere was energizing. He discovered that both women worked at the same salon in Dallas, thus their big hair and perfectly manicured nails. He told them he was a lawyer, leaving out the specifics, which they didn't seem interested in anyway. Kelsey and Tina were like the cover of a glossy magazine: their primary goal to attract attention. And that they did.

He received several envious glances from other men in the place and a few women too, but as the evening went on, he grew weary. Yes, they were nice to look at, but it wasn't enough. He kept getting distracted by thoughts of Callie and their earlier conversation in the pool.

His conservative next-door neighbor with her glasses, ever-present notepad, and curious glances seemed much more intriguing than these two women combined.

The evening took a turn for the worse when a band started playing and an area was cleared for dancing. He allowed himself to be pulled onto the dance floor, where Kelsey and Tina took turns gyrating against him. By then, they'd each had a few drinks and not much food, and the alcohol was taking effect.

He'd nursed two beers over three hours, and he barely felt anything except the beginnings of a headache and the urge to escape. In his head, he kept hearing Eric egging him on: "Come on, man. These women are into you. Go for it."

But as attractive as they were, and as easy as it might have been, he wasn't remotely tempted.

He recalled thinking, *What the hell's wrong with me?* and *I wonder what Callie's doing right now?* which was ridiculous because he hardly knew her. They'd only exchanged a few sentences, yet he found her more appealing than these two.

At one point, he left them on the dance floor, stating he had to use the restroom. Truthfully, he just wanted a break. Afterward, he'd gone back to their table instead of returning to the dance floor.

A couple of young guys approached the women and chatted them up, but then Kelsey and Tina turned and pointed at Chase, and their would-be suitors wandered off. Chase wished the women had ditched him for the other guys, because he was done.

When they came back to the table, flushed and slightly out of breath, he said, "Are you two ready to get out of here?" Using that phrase turned out to be his second mistake of the evening.

Kelsey's face lit up, and she replied, "Hell, yeah!"

"Me too," Tina said, her blue eyes twinkling.

Rather than breaking the news in the crowded bar, he led them outside and waited until they were in the car.

"Do you want to come back to our place?" Kelsey asked. Always the leader, she'd snagged the front seat before Tina could.

Tina leaned in from the back seat and said, "Yeah. It's still early."

"Uh, well..."

"Or we could go to your place. That's fine too," Kelsey inserted, misreading the reason for his hesitation.

Taking a deep breath, Chase prepared his arguments and gave himself a pep talk. *You're a lawyer. You can do this.*

"I appreciate the offer. I really do. But I'm kind of a one-woman man."

Neither of them spoke, and in the silence, he imagined Eric saying, "You idiot!"

"Seriously?" Tina asked.

"Afraid so."

"Then why did you spend the whole day with us if you didn't..."

"You're both beautiful, and I was flattered by the attention."

Apparently, saying that was mistake number three.

"Flattered?" Kelsey said incredulously. "Do you mean to tell us we wasted our last full day on the island because you were *flattered*?"

Tina dropped her hand from his shoulder and slumped down in the back seat. At that point, he wasn't sure if she was feeling dejected or drunk, but it didn't matter. He just wanted to go home and forget this had ever happened, or didn't happen in this case.

"We could have had our pick of any guy in that bar tonight. But instead, we were counting on going home with you!" Kelsey said, her nostrils flaring as her anger rose. She wasn't nearly as pretty with a scowl, but that could be said of most people.

"I'm sorry," he said for lack of anything better. "I thought I could do it, but it turns out I can't."

"What kind of man are you?" Kelsey shouted as they pulled into the resort parking lot.

He didn't respond, but Kelsey kept ranting until he stopped in front of their building. He'd insisted on picking them up instead of the other way around, and now he was glad. He wouldn't have wanted them to cause a scene in front of his unit, and if he were being honest, it was because of Callie.

She'd probably already formed a negative opinion of him from earlier at the pool, but he didn't want to make it worse.

"Thanks for nothing!" Kelsey spat. She hopped out of the car and then opened the back door for Tina, who, by the looks of her, might not even remember the episode in the morning.

"Good night," Chase said unnecessarily.

"Good riddance!" Kelsey replied.

He waited until they were safely inside before he heaved out a breath and drove away.

"What a disaster," he muttered as he let himself into his unit. But later, when he climbed into bed, he didn't feel guilty. He recalled Kelsey's question about what kind of man he was and came up with an answer.

He was a man of integrity. At least, that's what he strived for in all things. On the job, in his relationships, and especially with women.

That didn't mean he was perfect, and in his younger days, he might have jumped at the chance to be with Kelsey and Tina. But not now.

He wanted more than a meaningless fling. When the time was right for him to "get back out there," it wouldn't be with the Kelseys and Tinas of the world. He wanted a woman of substance. Someone who challenged him, intrigued him, and tied him up in knots for all the right reasons.

He'd had experience with arm candy, eye candy, and every other type of candy, and he was over it. *Sorry, Eric.*

The next time he got involved with a woman, it was going to be different.

And it's only going to be with ONE woman, he thought before he drifted off to sleep.

Chapter 9

Callie had written the first two chapters of her new novel when she stalled out again. She was sitting inside, hunched over her laptop, when Quinn called, and she welcomed the interruption.

"Aloha," she answered cheerfully.

"Aloha? You've been there for a week, and you speak Hawaiian now?" Quinn teased.

Callie laughed. She hadn't realized how much she missed her best friend until then. She'd been too busy spying on Chase and writing to think about anything else, but now she felt a twinge of homesickness.

"When are you coming to visit me?"

"As soon as I can swing it. So, what have you been up to? Meet any hot surfer dudes yet?"

Callie immediately thought of Chase, but she had no idea if he even knew how to surf. She was pretty sure he was talented at other things, though. At least, that's how she'd written his character.

"Not yet, though a surfer *dude* isn't really my type."

"What about your sexy next-door neighbor?"

"I haven't seen him for a few days."

"Bummer. From what you described, he sounds yummy."

"Well, he might be, but I'm not his type."

"Says who?"

"Says me. The last time I saw him, he was hitting on two women at the pool. For all I know, he's holed up with them somewhere." Even though she'd said it, she had trouble believing it, or maybe she just didn't want to.

"Maybe he was just being friendly."

"It doesn't even matter because I came up with a different use for him."

"Let me guess. You're writing him into one of your books."

"How'd you know?"

Quinn laughed. "Because I know you, and that sounds perfect. Whatever it takes to get you writing again!"

Callie sighed. "I wrote a couple of chapters, but now I'm stuck. I think I need to see him again to get some more material."

"Um-hmm."

"What?"

"Nothing. Just wondering if that's the *only* reason you want to see him again."

"Quinn. I barely know the guy."

"But you want to."

"For research purposes."

"Of course. What color are his eyes?"

"Green."

"Ah-ha! You answered that really fast."

"So what."

"So, you've studied him up close."

"Well, yeah. We were in the pool together."

"You were? Please don't tell me you were wearing your matronly bathing suit."

Callie cleared her throat but didn't reply.

"Dammit! I told you not to pack that one."

"He didn't seem to mind."

"What does that mean?"

She hesitated for a second, but Quinn was her best friend. She could tell her anything. "It was the strangest thing, but he kept looking at me even though he was there with two bikini models."

"Were they really?"

"I don't think so, but they could have been."

"Hmm. Maybe I underestimated the power of the black one-piece."

Callie giggled. "Anyway, we only talked for a few minutes before his *friends* pulled him away."

"And you haven't seen him since?"

"Not a glimpse... Hold on... I take that back." *Speak of the devil.* Chase had just come outside and was walking down the path toward the beach.

"Where is he? What's he doing?"

"Walking."

"Walking where? Go chase him!"

"I'm not going to *chase* Chase!"

"You have to for research. If not for that, for me. I'm living vicariously through you while you're in Hawaii."

"I don't want him to know I'm studying him. I have to be subtle about it."

"Subtle? You? Go after him, and the next time we talk, you better have written three more chapters!"

"Quinn."

"Bye. Love you!"

With that, Quinn hung up, leaving Callie standing there holding the phone and looking longingly out the window at Chase's retreating form.

She paced for a few minutes and tried to talk herself out of it, but in the end, she decided Quinn was right. She needed more interaction with him in order to keep writing.

So far, she'd written the meet-cute chapters of her novel, where the heroine and hero meet for the first time and sparks fly. Those were some of her favorite moments in any romance book, and she'd struggled to get them right. She strived to make her characters believable and likable and placed them in realistic situations.

She also liked building the anticipation before the characters became intimate, so she needed to write scenes with them interacting. In the past, she'd had daily interactions with Adam to draw from, but now...

"That's it! I'm doing it!"

She slid her feet into the flip-flops she'd left by the patio door, ran her fingers through her hair, and went out the door. This time, she didn't bother grabbing a notebook, because it would be too obvious.

She'd pretend she'd been out for a walk and had accidentally run into him. *And Quinn doesn't think I can be subtle. Ha!*

It was the hottest point of the day, and beads of sweat broke out on her back. She was wearing white shorts and a blue tank top with an anchor on it, and her hair whipped around in the breeze. Her skin was starting to brown, and she'd happily stopped wearing foundation since she'd lost her winter pallor.

It was amazing what one week in Hawaii could do for a person. She looked and felt better than she had in months. Feeling bolstered by her conversation with Quinn, she was glad she'd decided to track Chase down.

But when she got to the beach, he wasn't there. After scanning the sand, she looked out at the people swimming in the ocean, but he wasn't there either.

Then a giant splash made her turn to the left, where the sound had come from. There were ripples in the water, and then a man's head emerged, but it wasn't Chase. Her eyes traveled up to the cliff that he had apparently jumped from. There was Chase, standing at the edge, clapping along with a handful of other people who'd watched the man jump.

Her eyes bulged when she realized that he was in line to jump too. She was a writer, not a mathematician, so she had no idea how high the cliff was. However, it was high enough to make her stomach clench and to worry about his safety.

She spotted the path from the beach up to the clifftop and noticed a group of teens was currently traversing it. Her feet propelled her in that direction even though she had no idea what she'd do once she reached the top. All she knew was she wanted to get closer and watch the brave souls who were attempting it.

She took off her flip-flops and hurried across the sand. When she reached the dirt path, she stopped briefly to put them on again and wished she'd been wearing sneakers instead.

The path looked innocuous enough from the ground, but the more she climbed, the more she realized how high it was.

Don't look down, she chanted. Keeping her eyes straight ahead, she concentrated on placing one flip-flop in front of the other. *The things I do in the name of research!*

Once she reached the top, she paused to catch her breath and looked out at the magnificent view before her. If she'd thought the ocean was beautiful from the beach, this view was a thousand times better! Even if she hadn't been out of breath, the scene would have taken her breath away. Various shades of blue and green spread out as far as the eye could see, broken up by a few white puffy clouds and the whitecaps beating against the cliffs.

Just then, someone else jumped, and the onlookers cheered and clapped as the next person stepped up to take his turn. *Chase.*

"Chase!" It might not have been the best timing, but his name flew out of her mouth before she could stop it.

He jerked his head around and saw her, his expression a mix of surprise and pleasure.

"Hey, dude? It's your turn," said a teenage boy behind him.

"You go ahead," Chase said and stepped out of line.

He walked over to where she was standing slightly apart from the crowd and gave her a curious smile. "Hi."

"Aloha."

He chuckled. "I was surprised to hear my name. You almost missed me."

"Were you really going to jump?"

"Yeah. I've wanted to since I got here."

"But it looks so dangerous."

She assumed he'd already read the warning signs posted along the trail and at the top, though they'd obviously gone unheeded.

"I think it looks like a blast. You should try it."

She shook her head. "Risking my life for a quick rush isn't really my thing."

"But it could be the experience of a lifetime."

Just then, the teenager gave a loud victory shout as he disappeared over the edge.

"So, what are you doing here?" he asked, ignoring the activity around them.

"I...I was going for a walk, and..." *If only I could speak as well as I write!*

"And?"

"And I heard a splash, and when I looked up, I saw you."

"So, you decided to walk up the trail in your white flip-flops to say Aloha?"

Glancing down, she realized her flip-flops were more of a dusty brown color now. "I wasn't prepared."

"I see that," he said with a grin. "Did you think you'd be saving me from an untimely death?"

The word "death" instantly made her think of her grandma, but she quickly recovered.

"I was just curious. I guess I had to come and see for myself."

"Did you think I'd chicken out?"

She shrugged. "I don't know you that well."

"Well, since you're here, could you do me a favor?"

"Listen to your final confession?"

He laughed. "No. Would you mind holding my shirt and shoes while I jump? I was going to leave them here and walk back up, but maybe you could meet me down on the beach instead."

"Oh..." But he was already stripping off his shirt, and she was rendered speechless. She'd already seen him shirtless, but watching him undress was a whole other story. As the material slid up his stomach and then over his chest, she was treated to an up-close and personal view of his beauty. There wasn't an ounce of fat on him, and this was the same guy who had been eating a loaded Puka dog the other day!

His skin was tanned and smooth, and he had a contained patch of hair in two places, between his pecs and above the waistband of his swim trunks. She swallowed hard when he handed her his shirt, which was damp with sweat. Surprisingly, she didn't mind, and she accepted it like it was a Pulitzer Prize.

Next, he took off his rugged-looking sandals, but before he handed them to her, he said, "Do you mind?"

She shook her head, and he placed the sandals soles up on top of his shirt, presumably so she didn't have to touch them.

"I'm going to get back in line," he said, motioning over his shoulder. "You can watch if you want to."

"Okay," she replied, feeling nervous on his behalf. There were several people milling around, but most of them were watching rather than jumping. Peering over the edge, she got that awful sensation of falling and quickly stepped back.

"You don't have to do this, you know. It was brave of you to even consider it."

He laughed. "I'm doing this, Callie."

"Okay. Well, if I never see you again, it was nice meeting you."

"You too."

The next thing she knew, it was his turn to jump. He looked calm as could be, but her heart was pounding out of her chest.

"See you at the bottom," he said. He gave her a big smile and then catapulted himself off the cliff, tucking his legs up and wrapping his arms around them in a tight ball.

She watched him descend and hit the water with a loud splash, and she stayed there until his head popped up. He glanced up and waved.

She released a ragged breath and waved back, suddenly feeling ridiculously proud of him. Clutching his clothes to her chest, she went back down the path as quickly as she could since it was steep and she was wearing flip-flops.

She slipped them off once she reached the sand and hurried toward the shoreline, where he was waiting with some other guys who had jumped too. They were talking excitedly and exchanging high fives, and she smiled at their exuberance.

Chase looked happier than she'd seen him all week—even when he'd been flanked by two beautiful women at the pool. Then he turned and saw her and broke away from the others.

He trudged across the sand toward her, beaming. She wasn't foolish enough to believe it was because of her, but she was glad to have witnessed his shining moment.

"Great job! How was it?"

"Amazing! You really should do it."

"I'll leave the heroics to you, but I liked watching."

"Yeah?"

She nodded and handed over his things.

"I didn't even think to bring a towel," he said, looking down. He was dripping wet.

She trailed her eyes over him, trying not to pause too long in certain places. "You'll dry off on the walk back."

"Are you coming too? Back to your place, I mean."

She nodded. "I got plenty of exercise hiking up that cliff."

They turned and started walking back toward their building, falling into a comfortable silence. She assumed he was reflecting on his big adventure, and she was simply enjoying the day.

When they reached their units, she experienced a wave of awkwardness. Even though she hadn't jumped, they'd shared something, and she wasn't ready to say goodbye.

"Thanks for holding onto these," he said, holding up his shirt and shoes.

"No problem. I'm just glad I was able to give them back to you."

He laughed and started to turn away, but then he paused. "Hey. If you...if you're not busy...would you like to have dinner tonight?"

"Together?" *Duh!*

"Yeah. We can celebrate my surviving a potentially life-threatening jump."

How could she say no? Think of the research possibilities! "Sure. Dinner sounds good."

"Great. I'm going to take a quick shower. Can you be ready in half an hour?"

"Um-hmm."

"I'll knock on your front door when I'm done."

"Okay."

They went into their separate units, and the minute she'd closed the door behind her, she panicked.

"I'm going out to dinner with my muse! What if he asks about my job?" And if that thought wasn't terrifying enough, the next one was even worse.

"What on earth am I going to wear?!"

Chapter 10

Chase was nervous. You'd never have known he'd been out with two women just a few nights ago. He felt like a high schooler getting ready for prom instead of an accomplished lawyer going out for a casual dinner with his neighbor.

He wasn't sure why he felt the need to impress this woman, but he did. After his shower, he'd debated what to wear and chastised himself for acting like a girl. It wasn't like he had a slew of choices. He'd packed for Hawaii—shorts, T-shirts, a few collared shirts, khakis, and a few pairs of shoes. He finally settled on a lime green polo shirt, khaki shorts, and canvas slip-ons.

Next, he'd debated about wearing cologne. He'd used a masculine-scented body wash, but he thought cologne might be overkill. He decided to skip it, but he'd added an extra swipe of deodorant for good measure.

After he'd finished dressing, he grabbed his wallet, keys, and sunglasses and started to head out. But just before he opened his front door, he gave himself a pep talk.

It's just dinner. No big deal. You got this!

A few seconds later, he knocked on her door.

She opened it immediately, almost as if she'd been standing there waiting, and greeted him with a warm smile. He struggled to form words because conservative Callie was wearing a sundress that hugged her curves, brought out the rosy glow of her skin, and contrasted with her dark brown hair and eyes. She looked gorgeous.

"Hi," he finally said.

"Hi."

"You look nice."

"Thanks. So do you."

So far, so good. "Are you ready to go?"

"Um-hmm."

She stepped outside and turned to lock the door. Her sundress was held up by two thin straps, so her upper back and shoulders were mostly bare, and he found himself admiring her smooth skin.

He'd already noticed the smattering of freckles across her nose, and there were some on her back too. For some reason, he envisioned kissing them...

Then she turned around and almost knocked him over, he'd been standing so close.

"Oops," she said.

"Sorry," he said at the same time.

He couldn't be positive, but he got a sense that she was nervous too. Instead of making matters worse, the thought calmed him. *One of us has to pretend like we know what we're doing. Might as well be me.*

"Do you mind driving together?" he asked as they walked out to the parking lot.

She hesitated for a second and then replied, "Well, since I'm not sure where we're going, I'll drive with you."

He laughed, feeling more at ease by the moment. "I guess we didn't discuss that, did we?"

She shook her head, her silky dark hair glistening in the sun.

"What do you like to eat? Besides hot dogs, that is."

"I'm pretty easy. I mean, I'm pretty flexible. I mean..."

She cracked him up. "You're not a picky eater. I get it."

"Right."

"Have you been to Plantation Gardens? It's just a few miles up the road."

"No, but I read about it in my travel guide."

"I ate there a couple of nights ago. The food was delicious."

"I'm game if you don't mind going there again."

"Not at all."

"Okay. Let's do it!"

He tried to suppress a laugh, but she caught him, and her cheeks turned a pretty shade of pink. He was already having fun, and they hadn't even left yet!

He unlocked the SUV he'd rented and had wanted to help her in, but she beat him to it. Maybe she wasn't thinking of this as a date, which was fine by him.

"Have you explored much of the island yet?" he asked as they drove away.

"No, but I want to. What about you?"

"I went snorkeling the other day."

"How was it?"

"Great. Saw a lot of cool fish, some sea turtles, and a lazy monk seal."

"I've been meaning to do that too."

He gave her a sideways glance. "Is this a working vacation for you?"

She shrugged. "Sort of."

Her reserve only made him more curious. "Are you a reporter?"

She laughed. "No. Why?"

"Because just about every time I see you, you have a notebook and pen in your hands."

She studied him for a moment, like she was trying to decide something, and then she said, "I'm a writer."

"Ah. I knew it had to be something like that." But before he could ask what kind of writer, she moved on.

"What about you? What do you do besides hurl yourself off cliffs?"

He laughed. "I'm a lawyer, so it's kind of the same thing."

She giggled, and he liked the sound of it. There was nothing phony about this woman, and he found it refreshing.

"Do lawyers usually get eight weeks' vacation?"

"Technically, I'm on sabbatical."

"Sounds so formal."

"Goes with the job, I guess." Now he was the one being cagey, but he didn't really want to talk about work. "You never said how long you'll be here."

"I think we were interrupted by the Barbies."

"The Barbies?"

She looked out the window and shifted uncomfortably. "Sorry. I meant your friends at the pool."

"Oh. I get it. Well, we won't be interrupted by them anymore. They left the island."

Callie turned to look at him, and he swore he saw a flicker of relief in her eyes. Maybe it was just wishful thinking, though.

"Here we are," he said a few minutes later.

When he pulled into the parking lot, Callie's eyes went wide, and he was instantly glad he'd brought her there. The restaurant was surrounded by beautiful gardens, thus its name, and while he'd dined there alone the other night, it was much better suited for couples. Not that they were a couple, but still, it felt nice to have her company.

"This place is gorgeous," she said.

Instead of responding, he hurried and got out of the car so he could escort her up to the door. It might not be a date, but he was still a gentleman. She'd already opened her door, but he gave her a hand out, and she awarded him with a sweet smile.

He would have offered his arm, but she'd already started walking ahead, and he had to jog to catch up. *Why do I feel so out of practice?*

"Aloha. Would you prefer indoor or outdoor seating?" asked the pretty Hawaiian hostess.

Chase exchanged looks with Callie, and she said, "Outdoor, please."

He'd figured as much. The restaurant boasted a wraparound porch rimmed by tiki torches and a profusion of flowers. It was the perfect setting for a romantic dinner if one were interested in that sort of thing.

After they were seated and had given the waitress their drink orders, he picked up their conversation where they'd left off.

"You still haven't answered my question," he said lightly.

"Which one?"

"How long are you here for?"

"Oh, that one. Eight weeks, just like you. Well, seven now."

"How about that?"

She smiled and took a sip of water.

He got the sense that she was still holding back, and he wondered why. True, they didn't know each other that well, but talking was supposed to remedy that. Yet every time he asked a question, she looked uncomfortable and gave him clipped answers. Maybe she was out of practice with this too.

"I guess being a writer means you can work anywhere."

She nodded. "Have notepad and pen, will travel."

"You must make a decent living at it if you can afford to stay here for eight weeks." Based on her expression, he realized he'd offended her, and he could have kicked himself. "Sorry, I didn't mean to..."

"No. It's okay," she said, holding up her hand.

Just then, the waitress brought their drinks and asked if she could take their orders.

Since they hadn't even looked at the menus yet, Chase said, "Can you give us a few more minutes?"

"Sure. Take your time."

"I love that about Hawaii. Nobody's in a hurry here," Callie said, seemingly recovered from his previous comment.

"I agree. It's a lot different from where I live."

"Where do you live?"

"Michigan."

Her mouth dropped open, and she leaned forward, inadvertently giving him a peek down her dress. Not that he was planning on looking, but since the opportunity presented itself...

"Michigan?"

"Yeah. You know, the Mitten, the Great Lakes State...although it's not so *great* at this time of year."

"I know, I know. I live there too!"

His beer glass was raised halfway to his lips, and he halted in mid-air. "You're kidding me?"

She shook her head vehemently. "I live in Rochester."

"We're neighbors."

"Here or at home?"

"Both. I live in Troy."

"This is unbelievable!"

"I know." He took a long drink of beer and stared at her over the rim of his glass. What were the chances? It was like he'd walked right into a romantic movie or something.

"How long have you lived there?" she asked.

"All my life. You?"

"I was born in California, which was the impetus for my name. But my dad got transferred to Michigan when I was four, and I've lived there ever since."

"Wow. This is crazy. Of all…"

"The gin joints in all the world…"

"You show up at this one."

"I think we misquoted it," she said, laughing.

"Close enough."

"Are you a fan of *Casablanca*?"

"Not by choice."

She giggled. "Somebody forced you to watch it?"

"My sister."

"Older or younger?"

"Younger by a few years. What about you? Any siblings?"

"No. I'm an only."

She glanced down at the unopened menu then, bringing an end to the discussion. "We should probably decide, don't you think?"

He nodded and opened his menu, but inwardly he was still reeling over the fact that they lived so close to each other. They might have been in the same place at the same time back home and hadn't even realized it. Yet here they were, thousands of miles away, meeting for the first time.

"Everything looks delicious. I'm not sure what to get," she said.

He popped his head up and saw she'd put on her glasses to read the menu. He'd been so lost in thought he hadn't noticed her take them out of her purse. Her brow was furrowed, and she pushed the glasses further up her nose as she perused the menu. Why he found that sexy, he had no idea, but he couldn't tear his eyes away.

She looked up then and seemed surprised that he was staring at her. "Have you decided?"

"Not yet." He tipped his head back down and tried to concentrate on the offerings, but all he could think was, *I know one thing I want, and that's you.*

Chapter 11

Callie spent the next few minutes trying to tamp down her enthusiasm. Finding out that she and Chase were neighbors in Michigan had sent her reeling. It was good news on two fronts. First, it was possible they could maintain their friendship after their time in Hawaii was over, and second, she was going to incorporate this unexpected element into her book. She was almost angry at herself for not having thought of it before. Even better than falling for a stranger in an exotic location was the possibility of the relationship continuing afterward. It was perfect, really, and she could hardly wait to get back and start writing again. But first, she wanted to enjoy the rest of the evening with her muse.

"We could split the seafood platter," she suggested while they were perusing the menu.

"Sure," Chase said, closing his menu and pushing it aside. "So, tell me more about your life in Michigan."

It was a straightforward question, but she didn't have a simple answer for him. She was afraid anything she said would lead to topics she wasn't ready to discuss. On the other hand, it was a beautiful night, she was out to dinner with a handsome man, and so far, he'd been the perfect gentleman.

She took a deep breath and plunged in. "Up until recently, things were going great. But then I lost my grandmother late last year."

"Oh. I'm sorry to hear that."

"Thank you. We were really close, and I'm still trying to accept that she's gone."

"I get it."

She waited for him to elaborate, but he didn't. In the meantime, the waitress came over and took their order, giving her time to regroup. Talking about her grandma had caused a sharp pain in her chest, and she wondered when it would get easier.

"Did she live near you?"

"Yes. Just a few miles away, so I saw her all the time."

"Is that partly why you came here—to grieve?"

She nodded, but she wasn't ready to tell him the rest. "My family stayed at the same resort when I was in college, and my grandma came with us."

"It must bring back a lot of good memories then."

"Yes, but it's also a reminder that she's not here to enjoy it this time." Her voice cracked, and she picked up her drink as a distraction. Chase was so easy to talk to that she was afraid she'd spill everything if they kept this up.

"Do you mind if we talk about something else? I don't want to get all emotional and ruin our dinner."

He smiled. "Of course. It's your turn to ask me something."

"Okay. What made you decide to become a lawyer?"

He folded his hands and rested his chin on them, and she studied his face. His eyes were a pale green that looked almost gray in the dim light. His hair was close-cropped and medium brown with lighter streaks that might have been caused by the sun. He had a perfectly shaped oval face with thick brows, full lips, and light stubble along his jawline.

He was well-groomed, but she imagined he'd look just as handsome with messy hair, like when he first rolled out of bed in the morning...

"My dad owns a law firm along with two partners, so I became familiar with the business at a young age.

It was assumed that I'd follow the same career path as he did."

"Did you ever consider a different career?"

"Not really. I've always been interested in the law, although some of the shine has worn off. I'm contemplating making some changes when I go back home."

He didn't elaborate, and she decided not to push. Instead, she said, "Well, at least you can mull things over while you're lying in a lounge chair at the pool instead of back home in the freezing cold weather."

He gave her what appeared to be a grateful smile at the change of subject. "I know, right? My buddy Eric has been razzing me about it since I left."

"My friend Quinn too, but she plans on visiting while I'm here."

Just then their food arrived, and for the next several minutes, they didn't talk at all except to say, "Pass the ketchup," or, "The shrimp is delicious." While she'd been busy eating, he must have communicated to the waitress, because she brought them two more drinks.

Between the food, the cocktails, and the romantic ambiance, Callie was in heaven. But she reminded herself this wasn't a date—it was more of a working dinner. Besides, Chase hadn't given her any indication otherwise. He'd been polite, friendly, and a good conversationalist, but he hadn't flirted or hinted at anything else, and she was fine with that.

Like she'd told Quinn, she wasn't his type. He might like her as a neighbor or a friend, but she was more of a girl next door (literally in this case) than a girl you couldn't wait to get naked with.

Naked. Her? Chase? Together? She choked on a scallop just thinking about it.

"Are you okay? Here, drink some water," he said, handing her the glass.

She gulped it down and felt her face redden with embarrassment. "Went down the wrong tube," she said once she'd caught her breath.

"That'll happen."

Yeah. Especially when I'm thinking about you naked!

After they'd finished and passed on dessert, he said, "Do you want to take a walk through the grounds before we leave?"

"Sure. I'd love to see more of the gardens." *Plus, I'd like to spend more time with you.*

They paid the bill, which she insisted on splitting with him, and then went down the wide porch steps and onto the path that led to the gardens. It was dark, but tiki torches lined the pathways that wound in and out of various landscaped areas.

They strolled along, stopping occasionally to admire certain flowers that were indigenous to the area. They passed a few couples who were holding hands or who had stopped for a romantic kiss, and Callie decided this place was definitely going in her book. While she'd been soaking up the scene, she'd also been acutely aware of the gorgeous man by her side, and she'd noticed a few admiring glances from passersby.

They probably think we're a couple, she thought, *even though we're not doing anything coupley.*

"I just realized something. I never asked what kind of writing you do," Chase said, breaking into her reverie.

Her brain scrambled to come up with something that would be near the truth without revealing too much. "I'm a novelist, more of an aspiring one, really. I always feel like I'm *practicing* becoming a novelist."

"Kind of like me. They call it a law *practice* for a reason. You never really become an expert at it."

"Good analogy."

"So, the notebooks…"

"I find inspiration everywhere, so I always like to have one on hand."

"Do you have one with you tonight?"

"In my purse."

"Yet you haven't brought it out."

"I didn't want to be rude."

He chuckled. "Did you find anything inspiring?"

He'd stopped walking, so she did too. When she turned to face him, her breath caught. He was lit up from behind by a tiki torch, and his outline filled her vision. His hands were in the pockets of his khaki shorts, and his polo shirt stretched tight across his chest. That chest. She'd seen it enough times that she could envision every detail in her mind. He cocked his head, waiting for her response, and he might have been smirking.

"Yes," she said, her voice sounding a bit breathy.

He gave her a full-on smile then, and she practically melted. Something about being outside at night, surrounded by all this beauty, had her heart pounding. Or maybe it was because of the way he was looking at her like he was determined to figure her out.

She felt like they were playing a game of cat and mouse, but she was enjoying it. They were each revealing a little, but not too much, so the mystery was still there. Who knew she'd get this much material from one dinner out with him?

"Maybe we should head back," he said, but he didn't sound overly enthused about it.

She nodded because what else could she do? She hadn't wanted to suggest going to a bar because that might send the wrong message. Besides, she'd already had two drinks, and that was her limit. Any more and she might show all her cards. It was better to go home, write down some notes, and go to bed—alone.

They slowly walked back to his car, and this time, she let him help her in. It wasn't necessary, but she appreciated the gesture, and she liked the feel of her hand in his.

"So, what else are you going to do on the island besides write?" he asked on the drive back to the resort.

"I'd like to drive up the Na Pali Coast and check out some of the other beaches and towns."

"What a coincidence. I was thinking of driving up there too. Maybe we could go together one day."

"Oh."

He glanced over at her. "Or not?"

She laughed. "No, it's fine. I just didn't expect you to ask."

"Why not?"

Because I'm not your type? "Because we don't know each other that well?"

"Isn't that how you get to know someone? By spending time with them?"

"Yes…"

"You don't sound convinced."

"Sorry. I'm not very good at this."

"This?"

"The process of getting to know someone."

He'd pulled into the parking space in front of their condos and shut off the car, but neither of them made a move to get out. He shifted to face her, and she turned and met his eyes. Thank goodness she hadn't had a third cocktail. Who knew what might have come out of her mouth then?

"Am I making you uncomfortable?"

"No. You've been great."

"If you'd rather be alone, you can tell me. I'm a big boy. I can take it."

She shook her head and tried not to wonder how *big* he really was. "It's not that. I'm just surprised. I never expected to...make a friend while I was here."

He smiled. "Is that a bad thing?"

"No. I just envisioned being alone, that's all."

"Well, I don't know about you, but some things are better with company, like exploring the Na Pali Coast."

More book material, more book material... "You're right. I'll go with you."

"Great."

With that, they exited the car and walked up to their front porches, which were separated by a narrow wooden post. If this were a date, she might have expected a kiss, but since it wasn't...

"I had a really good time tonight," Chase said as she was inserting her key.

She paused and looked over at him. "Me too. Thanks for suggesting dinner."

"And you got some inspiration for your book."

She nodded and swallowed hard. *If you only knew…*

"I'm gonna hold you to that trip up the coast."

"Okay."

"And I know where you live, so don't think you can get out of it."

She laughed.

There was an awkward pause, and he took a step toward her, but she quickly pushed open the door. With one foot inside and one out, she said, "Goodnight, Chase."

"Goodnight, Callie."

After she shut the door, she leaned her back against it and breathed out. What on earth was happening? How had her research mission turned into what felt like a date and a promise of another one? This was crazy! This was supposed to happen to her book characters, not her!

A while later, she climbed into bed, thinking, *There must be some mistake. Is this life imitating art or art imitating life?*

Chapter 12

It rained on and off for the next few days—Hawaii's version of winter. Chase was mostly okay with it. It still beat snow. However, by the third day, he was getting restless. He kept wondering if Callie felt the same way, although she had her writing to keep her busy.

And that's when it struck him. She'd said she was an *aspiring* novelist, but if that were true, how had she afforded to stay here for eight weeks? He was no detective, but something didn't add up.

While the rain pelted the windows, he fired up his laptop and brought up Amazon. Then he hesitated for a moment, watching the cursor blink in the search bar. Why did he feel like he was infringing on her privacy? Writers wanted to be found, didn't they? How else would they sell any books?

Callie hadn't told him what kind of books she wrote—but why? Wasn't she proud of her work? He knew a few attorneys who had written books, and they tried to peddle them to him every time he saw them.

But she was different and much humbler than that. Still, his fingers hovered over the keys for a few more seconds. Ideally, he would have liked Callie to divulge more information about herself so he wouldn't have been tempted to spy on her.

"Ah, hell! I'm doing it!"

He chose the category *Books* from the drop-down menu and then typed in her first and last name. A long list of titles came up, but he wouldn't know which hers were until he saw the author's picture. A few of the titles were children's books, but he skipped those. He figured if she were writing stories for kids, she'd have nothing to hide.

There were also a few non-fiction books about obscure topics that he couldn't see her being interested in, so he skipped those too. Finally, his eyes alit on a book cover with a man and woman in a seductive pose—a romance novel. The title appeared at the top, and at the bottom were the words *By bestselling author, Callie Cooper*.

Could it be her? He clicked on the book to go to the product page and scrolled down until he found the author photo. *Bingo!*

There she was, her pretty face smiling back at him, wearing the same swingy hairstyle and glasses.

"Wow! Conservative Callie is a romance author." He clamped his hand over his mouth, remembering that she was right next door. Not that he'd heard much through the walls except for a few sounds that might have been her dropping something or shutting a kitchen cupboard. Still, he didn't want her to know that he'd discovered her secret.

Now that he'd found out, he was curious as to what type of romance novels she wrote. Maybe they were racy erotica featuring whips, chains, and ménages, and that was why she'd been so cagey about it. He couldn't quite picture it, though. But what was that saying—"It's always the quiet ones?"

He scrolled back up to the top of the page and read the book description. Apparently, this was book one of a series about three brothers and the women they loved. He'd never read romance before, but his sister had, and he'd seen similar books lying around the house. In fact, he used to tease her about them, and he'd even read a page or two until she'd whipped them out of his hands.

Does she still read them? Maybe she's even read this one!

He scrolled back down and read the section entitled *About the Author*. The description didn't tell him much more than he already knew; however, one sentence stood out: *Callie credits her grandmother for instilling the love of reading and inspiring her to become a writer.*

The words choked him up, and he remembered the look on her face at dinner when she'd talked lovingly about her grandma. He'd wanted to gather her in his arms then, but he couldn't. He hadn't known her well enough to make such an intimate gesture.

He understood she was still grieving the loss of her grandma, but he wondered if there was something else bothering her. So far, they hadn't discussed their love lives (or lack thereof), but he figured the topic would come up eventually.

She intrigued him, and finding out she was a romance writer only added to his curiosity. He flipped through a few more of her book pages and read snippets of readers' reviews. She'd written over ten books and seemed to have quite an avid fan base.

"Good for you," he said aloud. For some crazy reason, his chest swelled with pride. He'd always admired writers for their ability to put pen to paper and weave an engaging story. He'd love to pick her brain and ask her more about it, but now he'd created a dilemma.

If he admitted what he'd done, she might be angry and not want anything more to do with him. After all, she had her reasons for not telling him, and he'd gone behind her back—not an ideal way to start a new relationship. *Relationship? Really? Is that what you want?*

Sitting there, staring at her picture on the screen, he thought yes. Something about this woman had gotten under his skin, and he wanted to learn more. And not just about her career choice, but everything. But first, he'd have to convince her to open up to him.

While he'd been sitting there thinking with her book page on the screen, an idea struck him. *If I read one of her books, I might gain some insight into what makes her tick. It won't be spying so much as research, like when I'm working on a case. It's important to gather all the facts before I can properly represent someone. In this case, I'm the someone.*

He went back and scanned down her list of books, trying to decide which one to buy. Looking at the provocative covers with half-naked men and women, he said, "Thank goodness for eBooks!"

He couldn't imagine toting around one of these books for all to see. Come to think of it, maybe that was why so many women read on their e-readers or phones these days! Even his sister had recently switched to a Kindle. *Interesting...*

He picked up his phone, walked into the bedroom with it, and shut the door. He didn't want Callie overhearing through their shared wall even if it was only a remote possibility. But he had to run this by Miranda. She'd tell him what to do.

Glancing at his watch, he deduced it was the middle of the afternoon in Michigan, so it was safe to call. She'd have his head if he called at what she considered an "insane hour."

She answered on the second ring. "Aloha."

"I think I'm supposed to say that."

"What's up? I'm at work, remember?"

"Quick question. Have you heard of an author named Callie Cooper?"

"The romance author?"

"Yeah."

"Of course I have. I read her whole series. Why?"

Chase sat down on the edge of his bed and shoved a hand through his hair. "You're never going to believe this."

"Try me."

"She's here."

"Here where? There? At your condo?"

"Not *my* condo, but right next door. I met her. We went out to dinner."

"You're kidding me!"

"Why would I make that up?"

"I don't know. Tell me everything. What's she like? Is she as pretty as in her picture? I heard that authors doctor up their photos so they look younger."

Chase rolled his eyes. "She's actually prettier than her photo."

"Ohmigod. Are you...dating her?"

"No."

"But you went out to dinner."

"Yes, as neighbors and...friends."

"Hold up. You don't have any female friends."

"Well, I do now. Callie Cooper, the romance author."

"This is so cool! Wait until I tell..."

"Stop right there, little sister. You can't tell anyone about this."

"What? Why not?"

"Because she doesn't know I know, and I don't think she wants me to know."

"I'm confused."

He sighed. "Me too."

"Why wouldn't she want you to know?"

"Good question. That's partly why I'm calling. I need some advice."

"Hold on. I think we have a bad connection. You're asking *me* for advice?"

"Yes, smartass."

"Well, hurry up. I have to get back to work."

"If you were to recommend one of her books to someone, which would you choose?"

She was quiet for a moment, and he almost repeated the question, but then she said, "They're all good. Why do you ask?"

"Because I want to read one. I want to try to find out more about her, and I thought reading one of her books might help."

Miranda laughed, and it wasn't a giggle. It was a head-tipped-back, mouth-open-wide, squinty-eyed laugh. At least, that's how he pictured it.

"Forget it. I don't know why I asked," he huffed.

"Sorry. It's just hard for me to imagine you reading a romance book. They're quite different from crime novels, you know?"

"Are you going to give me a title or not?"

"Go with the first one in the series. It's a romance between neighbors, and it has a lot of witty banter and some steamy sex scenes. You'll like it."

Chase shook his head. *Neighbors? Interesting.* "Okay, but promise me you won't breathe a word of this."

"Only if you promise to keep me updated on your new...*friend*." She giggled this time.

"Why do I think I'm going to regret this?"

"Which part? Telling me or reading a romance novel?"

"Both!"

"My boss is giving me the evil eye. I gotta go. Love you."

"Love you too," he said, but she'd already hung up.

He went back into the living room and refreshed the screen on his laptop. There she was, still smiling at him. Before he could overthink it, he brought up the first book in the series and pressed the one-click button to buy it.

He was now the proud owner of his very first romance novel by none other than his *friend* and neighbor, Callie Cooper.

Chapter 13

Callie hadn't minded the rain. She'd made good use of her time indoors and written three more chapters of her new romance novel. Her main characters were in the getting-to-know-each-other stage, similar to her and Chase.

Chase. The man surprised and confounded her.

He looked the part of the sexy romantic hero, but in reality, he wasn't nearly as smooth and cocky as she'd imagined him to be. Confident, yes. Comfortable in his own skin, definitely. But not arrogant.

When she'd first observed him at the pool with the Barbies, she'd immediately assumed certain things about him. To an outsider, he looked like a typical playboy trying to score. But when she'd spent time with him at dinner, he hadn't acted like that at all. In fact, he'd seemed nervous at times.

A writer should know better than anyone not to judge a book by its cover. But that was exactly what she'd done with him. She'd been pleasantly surprised to discover there was more to him than met the eye. However, just like her, he seemed hesitant to reveal too much of himself. Why?

It shouldn't have mattered. She could still use him as her muse without knowing every last detail, but he intrigued her, and she wanted to learn more, which was why she was lying in bed at ten o'clock that night with her laptop propped on her legs.

"Why didn't I think of this before?"

She used Google constantly when she was writing, so why not now? She typed in his name, and sure enough, there were several hits for Chase Edwards in Michigan. She clicked on the name of his law practice, thinking that would contain the most accurate information.

On the home page, there was a group picture of all the attorneys in his office, and she picked out Chase and his dad right away. They were standing side by side, but even if they hadn't been, she would have known. His dad was an older version of Chase, with graying hair and a stouter build, but otherwise, they looked very similar. Chase was wearing a suit, and she studied him for a moment. Naturally, he filled it out to perfection just like everything else he wore. But this wasn't the Chase she knew.

This man was the consummate professional with a smile that didn't reach his eyes. He'd seemed disgruntled when he'd talked about his job, and she wondered why.

In the list of options on the screen, she saw one labeled *About our Attorneys*, and clicked on it. Then she clicked on his name. There was another picture of him at the top of the page, but the words beside it gave her pause—Chase Edwards P.C., Divorce Attorney.

She went on to read his biography, which included his schooling, years of experience, and designation as one of the top divorce lawyers in Southeast Michigan. After she read it, she shut down the laptop and placed it on the table beside her bed.

"A divorce attorney? Seriously? Of all the possible careers he could have, my romantic hero is a divorce attorney?"

Talk about opposite ends of a spectrum! How could a divorce attorney be a romantic lead when he spent his days helping couples break up? Did he believe in happily ever after? How could he after all he'd seen?

No wonder he was second-guessing his career choice. But why hadn't he told her? Was he ashamed or embarrassed? Had he been afraid it would turn her off? It wasn't the most appealing profession, but it could be worse. He could have been a stripper or a male escort... Hmm...not a bad idea for a future book.

Callie shook her head to clear her runaway thoughts. She had a bad habit of thinking beyond the book she was currently working on, which in this case was a good sign. It had been months since she'd been this immersed in a project. Her grandmother had known exactly what she needed, and she smiled at the thought of it.

She'd needed to escape her everyday life and gain a fresh perspective, and it was working. Discovering that Chase was a divorce attorney was a minor setback and could easily be remedied. Her book hero didn't have to be *exactly* like him. She could make him specialize in some other area of the law, but what? She didn't know enough about the profession to come up with an immediate solution. However, there was nothing to prevent her from picking Chase's brain on the subject.

Of course, she'd have to do so without arousing his suspicion that she knew what kind of lawyer he was. She'd simply act interested in the types of law that his practice specialized in, which would serve two purposes. One, it would give her more details for her book, and two, it might make him open up more.

She pretended that the first reason was more important than the second. But as she lay there trying to sleep, she thought more about Chase the man than Chase the book hero. Why was that?

She awoke the next morning with the sun streaming in through the slats of the blinds. When she got out of bed, she immediately opened them to see that the perfect Hawaii weather had returned. There wasn't a cloud in the sky, and if anything, the rain had only made the colors seem brighter.

While she was standing there, she noticed movement out of the corner of her eye and turned her head in that direction. It was Chase, jogging on the path that ran behind the condos and down to the beach, only he was heading in her direction.

She should have stepped back but decided not to. She had every right to be looking out the window at the gorgeous scenery—him included. Even if he saw her, she'd just smile and wave like a friendly neighbor would do.

As he came closer, he glanced over, but he was wearing sunglasses, so she couldn't be sure he'd seen her. He kept jogging, but he slowed down and then stopped in front of her window.

She started to raise her hand to wave, but he'd turned his back to her and bent down to tighten his shoelace.

"Wow," she mumbled and then swallowed hard. The man looked gorgeous from every angle, including this one.

"I bet the other lawyers in your office secretly hate you. Except the women," she muttered.

He slowly stood up and then performed a series of stretches. First, he tilted his head from side to side, and then he rolled his shoulders back a few times. Next, he punched his hands on his hips and twisted at the waist.

She watched every move, wondering if he went through this routine every time. It seemed like a shame not to watch. "If only you'd take off your shirt...and now he's doing it."

Still facing away, he slowly raised the hem of his T-shirt, revealing one inch of tanned, glistening skin at a time.

"If I didn't know better, I'd think he was giving me a show!" But she doubted he'd even seen her.

She admired him from the ground up—his muscular calves, tight buns, and tapered waist. His back muscles flexed as he whipped the shirt over his head and draped it over one arm.

While she was standing there gawking, she remembered writing a similar scene in one of her books. She'd written quite a few, so it was getting harder to remember which one. She smiled at the memory, and then Chase turned around.

She was caught! But rather than pretend like she hadn't seen him, she lifted her arm and waved, even though inwardly she was cringing. He waved back and then held up his index finger as if asking her to wait.

Wait for what? I'm in my pajamas! But Chase was walking straight toward her, and she felt trapped. The master bedroom was right next to the living room, and each had a sliding glass door with access to the patio. As he came closer, he motioned for her to step outside.

She glanced down at her pajamas and back up at his smiling face. They weren't anything special—just a two-piece knit set in pale blue that resembled a T-shirt and shorts. Still, she wasn't used to parading around in her pajamas in front of a stranger.

Only, Chase wasn't looking at her like a stranger at all. He perused her body from her bare toes to her bedhead until his gaze landed somewhere in the middle.

She turned away and scrambled to find her robe, but then she remembered she'd left it in the bathroom. He'd stepped onto her patio now, so she grabbed the flimsy crocheted blanket that was lying at the end of the bed and wrapped it around her shoulders.

The blanket was more decorative than useful, but it would have to do. It was fine for her muse to show off his body, but she hadn't planned on doing the same.

Adopting a nonchalant air, she unlocked the patio door, slid it open, and stepped outside to greet him.

"You're up early," she said a little too loudly.

"I went for a run."

"I see that." *Keep your eyes on his.*

"I wouldn't have bothered you, but I saw you standing there, so I thought I'd say hello."

"Well, as you can see, I just woke up, but hello."

He smiled. "I was going a little stir crazy these past few days. How about you?"

"Not really."

"Let me guess. You were writing."

And stalking you on Google. She nodded.

"Anything good?"

"I'd like to think so, but I never really know until the readers weigh in."

He cocked his head and studied her with a curious expression. "I have a feeling you're good at what you do."

"Why is that?"

"You seem very…focused."

"Thank you?"

He chuckled. "You know, I'd be happy to read a few pages of whatever you're writing. In case you want an opinion or anything."

She shifted uncomfortably and pulled the pretend blanket tighter around her, even though the air was already plenty warm. "I don't let anyone read my work until I've finished the first draft. But thanks for the offer."

"Maybe there's another way I can help."

She eyed him suspiciously and waited.

"We could drive up the coast today and do some exploring. Maybe you'll get some more inspiration for your story."

She hadn't thought they'd get together again so soon, but it wasn't a bad idea. That way, she could pick his brain about lawyer stuff. "Okay," she said, nodding.

"Yeah?"

"Um-hmm."

"Great. What time can you be ready?"

She didn't even want to think about what her hair looked like right then. "Well, I need to shower and eat breakfast..."

"We could grab some breakfast on the way."

"Are you always this chipper in the morning?"

He laughed. "Just anxious to get out and explore."

His enthusiasm was contagious, and suddenly she was anxious too. "Okay. Give me half an hour, and I'll be ready."

He smiled big and started to leave, but then he paused. "Don't forget your notebook. Oh, and you might want to bring your swimsuit too." With that, he winked and was gone, leaving her staring after him.

Chapter 14

Chase smiled as he stepped into the shower. When he'd seen Callie watching him through her window, he'd recalled the scene he'd read in her book and couldn't resist acting it out. It hadn't been the identical scenario but close enough. In her book, the heroine had been eyeing her neighbor as he'd jogged down the street in front of her house. He lived across from her, and when he got up to his front porch, he'd whipped off his shirt and turned around to find her staring at him out her window.

Chase hadn't planned on imitating the book character, but when he'd seen her standing there and she hadn't turned away, he'd decided to give her a show. He hadn't done it to be cocky, but he was confident in his appearance, and he hadn't minded stripping for her, especially since she seemed like such a rapt audience.

He'd half-expected to turn around and find her gone, but she'd surprised him by smiling and waving instead. He hadn't planned any of it, but when he'd walked over to say hello, he'd surprised himself by asking her out.

He wasn't sure she saw it that way, though. He wasn't kidding when he'd called her focused. She seemed more intent on writing her book than anything else, and damn if he didn't admire that about her. To have an occupation that you enjoyed and that consumed you (in a good way)—that was living the dream. He wished he could say the same.

Thinking of being consumed—that was exactly how he felt once he'd started reading her book. He'd gotten into bed with it and started reading it on his phone. It hadn't taken long, and he was hooked. Her writing style was engaging, and the characters were likable and relatable. Before he knew it, it was past midnight, and he'd still been reading. After the first steamy scene, he'd finally put down the phone.

The characters hadn't had sex, but they'd shared some sensual kisses with the promise of more to come. He'd been surprised at how his body had reacted while reading the scene. It was reminiscent of his teenage years, when he and his friends used to sneak *Playboy* out of his friend's dad's "hiding place."

He'd felt like he was doing something wrong back then, but he'd been too titillated to look away. As an adult, he wasn't supposed to feel guilty for reading a sexy scene, but that hadn't been the source of his guilt. It was sneaking the book behind the author's back instead of owning up to reading it.

But he figured Callie had her reasons for not telling him she was a romance author. Maybe after spending time together today, she'd open up more. Then he could admit he was reading one of her books.

He quickly showered, dressed, and packed a bag with his swim gear. He smiled again, recalling the look on her face when he'd suggested she bring a swimsuit. She was the complete opposite of the "Barbies" he'd hung out with at the pool. While they'd been more than happy to show off their bodies, conservative Callie wasn't so eager.

He'd like to tell her that she had a beautiful body (what little he'd seen of it) and to own it, but he doubted he'd get the chance. They were only here for a matter of weeks, and then he might never see her again. However, they did live near each other in Michigan...

Don't even go there! You barely know the woman, and this is just a vacation. All too soon, he'd be back at work, filing divorce papers and listening to sob stories about cheating, lying, deceitful spouses, and how love never lasts.

He'd seen and heard enough to believe that it was true. What started out with hearts and flowers ended up with arguments over Aunt Betty's antique dishes and Uncle Bob's coin collection. It didn't matter if the couple had been together five, ten, or fifty years; it was all the same.

"We fell out of love, we grew apart, he cheated, she cheated, he gambled all our money away, etc., etc." He'd heard the same refrains over and over. And those were the milder ones. There were also stories of alcohol and drug addiction and physical and emotional abuse. Those were the worst tales of all, and he'd had to steel himself to hear some of them.

Through it all, he'd done his job, gaining fair settlements for his clients and leaving a trail of "happy customers." Only he knew that most of them weren't happy at all, even when they were awarded large sums of money and got to keep Uncle Bob's coin collection.

He could hear his friend Eric's voice now: "Man, you've become a cynical SOB."

And it was true. He no longer believed in love the way he used to. Growing up, he'd witnessed his parents' love and that of a few other relatives, but now those examples were buried deep underneath the pile of crap he'd had to shovel.

While he found Callie attractive, intelligent, and witty, he didn't have any intention of forming a relationship with her beyond the next several weeks. But he wasn't opposed to enjoying her company as long as she allowed it. Besides, he wasn't required to share his sorry stories if he didn't want to. She didn't need to know that he didn't believe in happily ever after, and as a romance writer, she probably wouldn't want to hear it.

Talk about polar opposites! A divorce attorney and a romance writer walked into a bar... It sounded like the opening line of a bad joke. He shook his head and chuckled as he picked up his wallet, keys, and beach bag.

Today was about enjoying the glorious weather, magnificent scenery, and Callie's company, and he would leave it at that.

Chapter 15

Callie opened her door just as Chase was about to knock. Her crossbody bag was draped across her chest, and she had two other bags by her feet, packed and ready to go.

Chase took one glance at them and chuckled. "We staying overnight?"

Ignoring his flirtatious tone, she said, "I just wanted to be prepared for all possibilities." *But not that one!*

He picked up both bags before she had a chance to and winced when he stood back up. "What kind of possibilities are we talking about?"

She stepped outside and locked the door before following him out to his car. "One bag has my beach gear and a change of clothes. The other has binoculars, notepads, pens, and a few snacks."

Chase opened the hatch of the SUV and set the bags inside.

"Oh, and my Kauai travel guide with some pages marked," she added, reaching in and plucking it out of the bag.

He glanced at the book with all her yellow sticky notes poking out of it and laughed.

"You really are prepared!"

She shrugged. "I'm a detail-oriented person, and I like to know what I'm getting into."

"Hmm," he said as they got into the car.

She noticed he hadn't helped her in this time, and she was fine with it. This wasn't a date. They were just neighbors (here and in Michigan!) exploring the island together. No big deal.

Chase pulled out of the parking lot and onto the two-lane highway heading north. "Since you've already done a lot of research, where to first?"

"There's a beach at the end of this road called Ke'e Beach. According to the guide, it offers great views of the Na Pali coastline. On the way, I thought we could stop at a couple of towns, specifically Princeville and Hanalei."

Chase eyed her with amusement.

"What?"

"I'm impressed with your research skills."

"As a lawyer, you must have them too." She saw his shoulders stiffen and realized it was a sore subject.

"I think you might have me beat."

"It's part of my job. I can't write about things I don't know, so I have to look them up. Google is one of my best friends."

He laughed. Then he pointed up ahead to a small café advertising *Good Eats*. "Ready for breakfast?"

"Sure."

They went inside the crowded restaurant and were seated at a cramped table for two. After they both ordered eggs, toast, and coffee, Callie decided to try and pick his brain again, but he beat her to it.

"So, how does it work? How do you come up with your stories?"

She hadn't planned on talking about herself, but he seemed genuinely interested. And if she divulged more about herself, he might reciprocate.

"While I'd like to say there's a method to it, there really isn't. The stories just sort of come to me, and then I feel compelled to write them."

"What about the characters? Do you base them off real people?"

She shifted in her chair, accidentally bumping his knee under the table. "Sorry."

"No problem," he said with a smile.

Suddenly she'd become the interviewee instead of the interviewer, and she wasn't entirely comfortable with his line of questioning. "Why do you ask?"

"Just curious. I've always admired writers, and I'm interested in the process."

She took another sip of coffee and tried to calm herself, though a heaping dose of caffeine probably wouldn't help. "The characters are *mostly* imagined; however, I have incorporated bits and pieces from people I've known."

"Interesting. Like who? Boyfriends?"

She'd been raising the coffee cup to her lips, and she paused with it in mid-air.

"I wouldn't know any of these people, so it's safe to tell me, right?"

Just then the waitress brought their food over giving her a brief reprieve. "Can I get you anything else?"

They both shook their heads, and the waitress walked away.

Callie speared a bite of scrambled egg and avoided Chase's eyes. She chewed thoughtfully while he spread neat rows of strawberry jam on his wheat toast. If she thought he might forget where they'd left off, she'd been wrong.

"So, about your characters?" he said before taking a large bite out of his toast.

She watched him chew and noticed the smudge of strawberry at the corner of his lips. If this were a scene in one of her books, she would reach over, wipe it off, and then suck it off her finger. Or if the characters were further along in their relationship, she might lean across the table and lick it off...

"Callie? Where'd you go?"

She shook her head to get rid of her wayward thoughts. "Just enjoying the food."

"If you'd rather not talk about your work, that's fine. I was just making conversation."

She suddenly realized how ridiculous she was being. "I had a long-term relationship, and yes, it provided some inspiration for my books. But I also get inspiration from other sources."

Chase nodded like he knew it all along. "*Had*, as in past tense?"

Why is he so curious about this? "Yes. We broke up a few months ago."

"Did you kill him off? In your book, I mean."

"No, but I thought about it."

He chuckled.

"Anyway, I don't write murder mysteries, so I couldn't kill him off."

He looked like he was about to ask another question, but then the waitress came over with their bill.

Callie reached for her purse, but Chase was quicker, and he handed the waitress his credit card.

"I should pay since you're driving," she said even though she appreciated the gesture.

"I would have made the drive anyway."

"But you wouldn't have bought two breakfasts."

"If you ever give up writing, you could be a lawyer. You sure argue like one."

She laughed. "I'll buy lunch."

"Fine," he said and followed her out of the restaurant.

For a while, they drove in silence, and Callie looked out the window at the passing scenery. Kauai was a vision in greens and blues, and it was raw in its beauty. It had an untamed ruggedness compared to other tropical places she'd been to, and she loved that about it. She also liked the absence of busy cities. Instead, there was a smattering of charming small towns that blended in with the natural surroundings.

For long stretches of the drive, there was virtually nothing but dense green growth crowding the highway, and they only passed a few cars. It struck her that she'd put her trust in this man who was a virtual stranger. She was thousands of miles from home, and nobody knew exactly where she was or who she was with. If she were a mystery author, this would be the setup for the perfect crime.

She studied his profile as he drove, thinking he wouldn't notice. If only she could take out her notebook, then she'd be able to fill in a few more details about his appearance and demeanor. But that would be too obvious. Instead, she'd have to take mental notes and write them down later.

Chase looked over and caught her staring. "Hi," he said with a grin.

"Sorry. I was just thinking."

"About your book?"

She nodded.

"Come up with anything good?"

"I have some ideas."

"If you want to run them by me, I'd be happy to listen."

She eyed him curiously, wondering why he seemed so interested in her writing. "Thanks, but they're just random thoughts at this point."

"Well, if there's any way I can help, just let me know. I'm right next door."

The way he looked at her when he said it made her squirm. Suddenly it didn't sound like he was talking about her book anymore…

Chapter 16

He hadn't meant to flirt with her, but it was so easy to do. He liked the coy smile she sometimes got and the look she'd given him—like she'd known what he was up to and didn't altogether mind. After finding out that she'd had a long-term boyfriend and they'd recently broken up, he suspected she hadn't been flirted with in a while and maybe she'd missed it.

Now he was waiting outside the restroom for her at Ke'e Beach, and he told himself to rein it in. He wasn't opposed to some harmless flirting if it didn't go any further than that.

But a few minutes later, when she came out of the restroom where she'd changed into her swimsuit, he did a double take. He'd assumed she'd be wearing the same conservative one-piece he'd seen her in last time—wrong.

Today she was wearing a floral-print bikini with a ruffle on the top and bottoms. It was still demure as bikinis went; however, he suspected it was daring for her. She was holding her beach bag in front of her like a shield, but he'd seen enough to be titillated.

"Ready?" she said with a tight smile.

Dammit. I made her self-conscious. "You look great," he blurted out, attempting to make her feel more comfortable.

"Oh. Thanks."

"Want me to carry your bag?"

"No. I got it."

They trudged across the sand until they reached a spot that offered an unobstructed view of the jagged cliffs lining the coast. By unspoken agreement, they stopped and spread out their towels before plopping down on them.

It wasn't even noon yet, but the beach was humming with activity. There were women of all shapes and sizes wearing a lot less than Callie was, but Chase couldn't stop looking at her. This time, though, he tried to be more discreet.

Just when he'd thought he'd figured her out, she'd surprised him again. He leaned back on his elbows and watched her take the sunscreen out of her tote bag. If he were one of the heroes in her books, he'd offer to rub it on her, but as it was, he didn't think she'd be receptive to it.

He contented himself with sitting back and watching as she massaged the lotion into her skin one beautiful square inch at a time. He was wearing sunglasses, so he figured he could get away with it.

She started on her left arm, which was closest to him, and he saw her slim fingers glide over her freckled skin. *Freckles—maybe that's why she's being so diligent.* Instead of ogling her, he should have been applying sunscreen too, but he didn't want to miss a thing.

After thoroughly coating both arms, she moved on to her neck and chest, and he shifted on the towel. She tilted her head up and ran her hand down her neck before spreading the lotion above her bikini top. It was almost like she'd forgotten he was there, and she dipped her hand slightly under the top edge, giving him a brief glimpse of cleavage.

He felt a twitch in his swim trunks and suppressed the urge to cover himself with his hands. But doing so would only draw her attention there, and he didn't want her to know he was aroused. So, he stayed very still and hoped she wouldn't notice.

Now she'd moved on to her midsection, and he sat up a little more to answer the burning question—innie or outie? *Innie. And she's moving on…*

He was glad she didn't dip her hand under the waistband of her bikini bottoms, because he might have had a heart attack. He was already breathing heavily as it was. But Callie seemed completely oblivious to his discomfort. Her laser focus was in place, and she didn't even acknowledge his presence. Right then, given his state of arousal, he was glad.

She poured some lotion into her left palm and started smoothing it down her left leg, bending forward to reach her toes, which he noticed were polished a bluish-green color kind of like the ocean. He'd bet his life savings that she'd done it on purpose. In her words, she was "detail-oriented," and he'd guess she'd wanted to match her polish to the environment. He smiled at the thought of it.

She repeated the process on her right leg and then started to put the lotion away but paused. "Do you need to borrow this?"

It took him a second to find his voice. "Nope. I brought some."

"Aren't you going to put it on?"

"I already have a good base, and I don't usually burn."

"Lucky."

He shrugged. Truthfully, he should have put some on, but he'd been too busy watching her, and now he felt stupid.

She slipped the lotion into her bag and pulled out a Kindle. Holding it up, she said, "Mind if I read for a little bit?"

He chuckled, not because she wanted to read, but because she really had thought of everything. "Be my guest. I'm just going to lie here and close my eyes for a few minutes."

"Okay."

He lay down and cradled his head in his hands, but he didn't immediately close his eyes. Instead, he watched Callie fold up a smaller towel and place it under her head to use as a pillow.

Finally, she lay beside him (their towels were close but not touching) and sighed.

"You good?" he asked with a hint of amusement.

But she didn't miss a thing. Turning her head toward him, she said, "Something funny?"

"No," he said unconvincingly.

"Come on, what is it?" She propped herself up on her side and looked down at him.

"I just enjoyed your little routine, that's all."

"My little routine?"

"Yeah. You're very...thorough."

"Somehow that doesn't sound like a compliment."

He tipped his sunglasses down to better see her face and saw she was smiling. There was hope for him after all.

"I think it's cute."

"Ugh," she said and lay back down in a huff.

He sat up and looked down at her, trying to keep his eyes on her face and not roaming down the petite length of her beautiful body.

"Something wrong with the word 'cute'?"

"It's a word I'm overly familiar with, that's all. It describes puppies, kittens, and short people."

He opened his mouth to say something, but she suddenly sat up. Apparently, she had more to say on the subject.

"For example, you probably wouldn't use the word 'cute' to describe the Barbies. They'd be referred to as sexy, svelte, or hot, but never cute."

"I have to argue with you."

"Because you're a lawyer," she huffed.

"No. Because I'm a man, and I disagree. First off, cute is not a derogatory term. Second, I would never use the term *svelte* to describe anyone. And for my closing argument, you're damn sexy, but I didn't think you'd appreciate me saying so."

He was met with dead silence, and her mouth hung open in surprise. Frankly, he was surprised too. He hadn't meant to go there, but it was out now, and he'd have to deal with the consequences.

"Well?" he said when he couldn't take it anymore. Might as well rip off the bandage all at once.

"You think I'm *sexy*?"

Uh-oh. He wasn't sure which way this was going to go, but he forged ahead. "Yes, I do. And it doesn't matter whether you're wearing a black one-piece bathing suit and a cover-up or a bikini. Hell, you could probably wear a burlap sack, and I would still think it. So, there you have it. Full confession. Guilty as charged." He held up his hands in surrender but quickly lowered them, thinking he was acting like a dramatic courtroom lawyer on TV.

He waited for the fallout, counting down the seconds in his mind and preparing himself for the end of their short-lived friendship. But instead, she reached over and placed a hand on his arm.

Looking him straight in the eyes, she smiled and said, "Thank you."

Chapter 17

Thank you? Really? She'd been so flabbergasted she hadn't known what else to say. Chase Edwards, her book hero, thought *she* was sexy. She hadn't seen that coming!

When she'd decided to bring the bikini (that Quinn had helped her pick out), she'd been nervous about wearing it with him. If she had been on her own, she'd have minded less because she'd never see the other beachgoers again and she didn't really care what they thought. But with him, it felt different.

While they were spending time on the island together, she cared what he thought. She'd already memorized what he'd said so she could use it in her book. She liked how the compliment had slipped out almost by accident and that he'd sounded apologetic, like he was afraid of her reaction. She found the entire scene utterly charming.

Now he was lying back, relaxing in the sun with his eyes closed. But for some reason, she doubted he was sleeping. If only she knew what was going on in his head. Then again, she liked the anticipation. Who knew what might come out of his mouth next?

For a while, she tried to concentrate on reading. She'd loaded her Kindle with several romance novels before she'd left home, thinking that even if she were writing again, she'd still have plenty of time to read. But she'd never expected to be spending her time with someone else, especially a man.

She was distracted with Chase lying so close, and she kept sneaking peeks at him. She watched his chest rise and fall as he breathed, and then she trailed her gaze down his long length. His very presence stirred her and made her feel things she hadn't felt in a long time.

Finally, she gave up on reading and sat up to slide her Kindle into her bag. The movement must have roused Chase because he sat up too.

"Did I wake you?"

"I was just resting."

"I was thinking about cooling off." The water looked inviting, and she at least wanted to get her feet wet.

"I'll come with you."

"Okay."

They walked down to the water's edge, and Callie noticed a few heads turn in his direction, but he seemed oblivious. She felt a burst of pride that she was there with him, even if it was misguided. They weren't a couple, and they could barely be called friends. Still, she enjoyed being with him.

They waded into the water until it was up to her knees, and she looked down at a colorful school of fish swimming by. When she glanced back up, she saw that Chase was further out and immersed up to his neck. He caught eyes with her and smiled.

Talk about sexy. Does he know it?

He crooked his index finger at her, motioning for her to come and join him. While she enjoyed swimming in pools, she was always a bit trepidatious about swimming in the ocean, especially here, where she knew the undertow could be strong and dangerous. However, this beach had two lifeguard stations, and it made her feel safer. Truthfully, it had been part of the reason she'd chosen it, but she hadn't told him that.

Looking around and seeing all the people in the water laughing and splashing made her worries disappear, and she started moving toward him. She hadn't expected the quick drop-off, though, and it caught her off balance. She plunged headfirst into the water and came up sputtering.

She reemerged to see Chase laughing. "You didn't warn me about the drop-off," she accused once she'd reached him.

"Sorry. I thought you'd see it."

"I was looking at you." *Great! Why'd you just admit that?*

"Really? I'm flattered."

"Don't be. I was just trying to judge how deep it was." She was standing on her tiptoes with her head above water, but one wave and...

It was like she'd conjured it up, and the next thing she knew, she slammed right into his hard chest. His arms immediately went around her waist, and he held on tight. She gripped his shoulders and clung to him. After the wave receded, she relaxed some, but he still didn't let go.

"Are you okay?"

At this proximity, it was impossible to think straight, let alone form a complete sentence. Their bodies were touching from shoulders to hips, and she felt every hard ridge of him pressing against her. This was another time when she didn't mind being petite. She felt safe and protected with his large, strong body wrapped around her. But she felt something else too as evidenced by her hard nipples.

"Callie?"

"Yeah. I'm fine. Just startled."

"Me too," he said, but she got the sense he wasn't talking about the wave.

"You can let go of me now."

"I don't think so."

She gaped at him and stared directly into his striking pale green eyes. They really were an unusual color. She wasn't just making that up for her book. "Why not?"

"I'm afraid you'll go under, and I can't let that happen."

She cocked her head and studied him, trying to ascertain if he was joking. But he looked dead serious—unless this was his lawyer face, the one he used to intimidate people in the courtroom.

The waves were gentler now, and he loosened his grip some. Glancing down at his shoulders, she said, "I left red marks."

"It was worth it."

His palms were warm on her bare waist, and his leg hair tickled her thighs. She eyed him warily. "Are you flirting with me now?"

"Would that be so horrible?"

"Answering a question with a question. Isn't that what lawyers do?"

He chuckled. "When will you stop seeing me as a lawyer and start looking at me as a man?"

I already do. "Why does it matter?"

"This conversation could last all day."

"Would that be so horrible?"

"Touché," he said, laughing.

Just then another wave slammed her into him again. Even if she'd been trying to keep her distance, Mother Nature had other intentions.

His arms tightened around her. "Good thing I was still holding on."

"I'm not so sure."

"You could let go if you really wanted to."

She couldn't argue with that. "Why are you here, Chase?" This was the closest they'd been physically, and now she hoped he'd open up emotionally.

He sighed, his breath tickling her neck and making her shiver.

"Are you cold? Do you want to get out?"

"You're avoiding my question."

"You've avoided mine too."

She shook her head. "I told you about my grandma, my ex, and my job. What more do you want to know?"

He stared at her for a few beats but didn't respond. He was closing down on her, and she was dying to know why.

"Why do you do that? You share something, and then you go silent. You seem to want to know me, but you don't want me to know you."

"We're only here for a short time, Callie. Why do we have to know everything?"

At some point while they'd been talking, she'd slid her hands from his shoulders down to his biceps, which were hard and unyielding. He seemed to be acting the same, and she let go, feeling the loss immediately.

"I want to get out now," she said, crossing her arms over her chest.

He nodded and dropped his hands from her waist.

She turned and waded away, aware that he was right behind her. As soon as she returned to their spot, she picked up her extra towel and wrapped it around her while Chase simply sat down on his.

She took her time drying off before sitting down beside him. His arms were wrapped around his knees, and he was staring out to sea, seemingly lost in thought. She wished she hadn't pried, but she'd gone into writer mode, trying to wring every emotion out of him even though he wasn't ready to share them.

"I'm sorry," she said softly.

His head whipped around. "For what?"

"For trying to analyze you instead of just hanging out."

His lips quirked up, but his smile didn't meet his eyes. "You were in writer mode."

"When will you stop seeing me as a writer and start seeing me as a woman?" she teased, borrowing his words from earlier.

He shifted his body to face her and met her eyes. "I do see you as a woman, Callie, and that's part of the problem."

Chapter 18

Their conversation was stilted on the way back to the resort, and Chase wasn't sure how to fix things. "Do you want to stop for lunch?" he asked as they approached the town of Hanalei, which she'd mentioned earlier.

"I'll take a rain check. I feel dirty after the beach, and I'd like to go home and clean up."

In his opinion, she looked gorgeous. Her hair fell in natural waves rather than the usual tamed tresses. Her skin was sun-kissed, and the freckles across her nose looked even more pronounced. She'd changed back into shorts and a T-shirt, and he admired her bare legs and blue painted toes in her flip-flops. He'd like to tell her she looked perfect the way she was, but he'd already crossed the line today. Any further, and he'd be knee deep in quicksand.

He wasn't sure how it had happened, but when she'd fallen into him in the water, he hadn't wanted to let go. She'd surprised him again when she hadn't tried to break out of his hold. He'd relished the feel of her soft curvy body against his and the way she'd clung to him like he was a safety net. Whether from the cool water or from the close contact, he'd felt the hard points of her nipples pressing into his chest. He'd already been aroused on the sand, but then his desire had flared, and he'd fought to keep it in check.

Had it been any other woman, he might have kissed her, but with Callie, he was cautious, partly for her sake but also for his. He enjoyed her company too much to risk their burgeoning friendship or whatever it was. But it hadn't felt like friendship when he'd been holding her in his arms and sporting an erection.

Now she sat stiffly in the passenger seat, gazing out the window, and it felt like she was a million miles away. He blamed himself for that. If only he'd been more open and answered her questions. Then they might still be enjoying the day and maybe even the night...

"If I ask you something, will you answer me this time?" she said, startling him.

"Go ahead," he said cautiously.

"What did you mean when you said it's a *problem* that I'm a woman?"

He almost laughed but caught himself. This time, he felt compelled to give her an honest answer.

Otherwise, she might not give him another chance, and he didn't want that to happen.

"That's not quite what I said."

"You know what I mean."

"Yes, and you deserve an answer, though you may not like it."

"That's okay. I can take it."

He shot her a glance and saw the look of determination etched on her beautiful face. There was no way he was getting off easy. "What I meant is that you're an attractive woman and I'd be a fool not to notice."

"But..."

"But I didn't come to Hawaii to get involved with anyone."

"So, how do you explain the Barbies?"

"That was a harmless flirtation, and to be honest, it was good for my ego."

"Your ego seems perfectly healthy to me."

He frowned, and she visibly softened.

"Sorry. I didn't mean to sound so snarky."

"Apology accepted. Here's the bottom line: I recently went through a bad breakup, and I'm not interested in another relationship. I came here to escape my life for a while and to rethink some things, not start up with someone else."

"Meaning me?"

"Meaning anybody, the Barbies included. And for the record, nothing happened with them. They propositioned me, but I turned them down."

"Ouch."

"Yeah. The Barbies weren't happy about it, and they had a few choice words for me before they left. But I couldn't do it. I discovered I'm a one-woman man."

"Hmm."

"Are you surprised?"

"I have to admit that when I first met you, I figured you'd jump at the chance, but now..."

"Yes?"

"You're different than I originally thought."

"Different good or different bad?"

She smiled for the first time since they'd left the beach, and he felt his shoulders relax. He wasn't sure why it was so important that she liked him, but it was.

"Different good. But you should know that I'm not looking for a relationship either. I came here at my grandmother's urging to give my writing a jumpstart. Between my break-up and her illness, I got away from it for a while. So, the fact that I'm a woman doesn't have to be a problem. We can be friendly while we're here, but I don't want or expect anything outside of that."

Mind blown. Coy Callie wasn't afraid to speak her mind, and her words packed a punch. He should have been relieved, but somehow he felt disappointed instead. They both wanted (or didn't want) the same things, and now that they'd laid it out there, everything should be easier between them. Yet why did he feel the urge to take it all back?

"Are we good now?" she asked, her eyes shining with hopefulness.

"We're good." But if he'd been in a courtroom in front of a jury, he doubted they'd be convinced.

When they got back to the resort, Chase took her bags out of the back and brought them up to the porch.

"Do you want me to carry them inside for you?" Now that they were home, he was reluctant to leave her.

She shook her head. "I'll take them."

While he was transferring the bags to her hands, she went up on her tiptoes and kissed his cheek, shocking him once again.

"What was that for?"

"A friendly thank you for today. I had fun."

"Oh. Well, you're welcome."

She smiled exuberantly, and he pondered the sudden change in mood.

"I'm so glad we talked. I feel a lot better now."

And there was his answer. Too bad he didn't share her enthusiasm. If only he'd turned his head slightly when she'd gone to kiss his cheek. Then she might have landed on his lips instead.

"Yeah. Me too."

"Okay, then. I guess I'll see you around."

She started to turn away, but he hadn't budged. He was standing there like an idiot, trying to think of something else to say, when she turned back around.

"Chase?"

"I...um...I was just thinking about the sunset."

She glanced up at the bright blue sky and raised her brows in confusion. "It's only mid-afternoon."

"Yeah, but I heard the sunsets here are spectacular, and I haven't seen one yet."

"Oh. Me either."

"Would you like to get together and watch it sometime?" He hadn't been this nervous since he'd asked Emily Rockwood to homecoming in tenth grade. What in the hell was wrong with him?

"That sounds good, but not tonight. I have a lot of writing I want to do."

He nodded. "I understand. Another time, then."

"Sure. Have a good night."

"You too."

With that, she turned and went inside, leaving him standing on the porch and feeling sixteen years old.

Chapter 19

For the next few days, Callie wrote furiously, the words flying off her fingertips and onto the page. She couldn't believe how much material she'd gained from her last outing with Chase. She'd even used their physical encounter in the water to write her first sexy scene between the characters. She'd tweaked it so the hero and heroine shared their first kiss, and it was electric. In reading it over, she'd gotten tingly, which was a sign that her writing was on point. If she'd reacted that way to her own story, she felt assured that her readers would too.

She could practically kiss Chase for giving her the inspiration. But after their discussion in the car, she knew that kissing was out of the question. That hadn't stopped her from daydreaming about it, though. Before she'd written the kissing scene in her book, she'd closed her eyes and recalled how it felt to be in his arms with the sun beating down and the water lapping around their bodies. He'd held her firmly yet gently, and he'd gazed at her with a mixture of sweetness and desire that had warmed her to the core.

When the waves had knocked her into him, she'd brushed up against the front of his swim trunks and could have sworn he'd been hard. She'd been shocked to elicit that kind of reaction in him when they hadn't even kissed, but the incident had given her plenty of material to work with, and she'd written four more chapters as a result.

After she'd been holed up writing, she felt the need for a break. She'd barely left the condo except to get food, and she'd only spotted Chase once when he'd been walking down the path toward the beach. He'd glanced up at her unit, but she'd been sitting far enough away from the window that he hadn't seen her. She'd watched him until he was out of sight and had even considered going outside to join him. But she'd stopped herself. She hadn't wanted him to think that she was constantly on the lookout for him because she wasn't. But today she considered seeking him out.

She could use some more material for her book, but she also missed his company, so that evening she decided to take the initiative and ask him out to dinner. Now that they'd established their friendship, she wouldn't have to worry about him taking the invitation the wrong way. If they'd exchanged phone numbers, she would have called or texted, but since they hadn't, she walked outside and knocked on his front door.

When he didn't answer, she turned and looked for his car. When she saw it was in the parking lot, she knocked again.

This time, he answered, and he gave her a broad smile. He was shirtless and wearing a pair of light gray athletic shorts that hung low on his waist. She'd seen him shirtless several times before, and it was still a sight to behold. But what she hadn't seen was him wearing glasses—tortoiseshell frames that showcased his magnificent green eyes.

While she wore glasses too, she considered them a necessary evil rather than a fashion statement. But Chase in glasses was seriously hot!

"Hey," he said. "Come on in."

She stepped inside even though she could have asked him to dinner on his porch. But she was curious about his "space" and wanted to see what she could glean from it.

"Finally emerged from your writing cave, huh?" He motioned her into the living room, and she took a seat on the couch.

Glancing around, she saw that his unit had the same layout as hers, but it was decorated differently. She also noticed that other than a large stack of books on the dining room table, there weren't any other personal items lying around.

"Doing a little light reading?" she said, pointing to the books.

"I've been doing a lot of reading on this trip."

"I can see that."

"So, what brings you by?"

He leaned forward and clasped his hands in front of him, looking cool and casual. In that moment, she felt exactly the opposite. Her hands were clammy, and she suddenly felt shy. But she went ahead with her plan.

"I was wondering if you were free for dinner tonight?"

A flicker of surprise crossed his face, but he smiled and said, "Sure."

"Great. Maybe we can catch the sunset afterward."

"Sounds perfect."

"Okay, then. It looks like you might need a few minutes to get dressed, so I'll just wait at my place." She started to rise, but he motioned her to stay seated.

"Wait here. I'll be right back."

He shot off the chair and disappeared down the hall to his bedroom, leaving her alone to catch her breath.

Instead of sitting still, she got up and wandered over to the dining room table to peruse his book choices. She saw titles by James Patterson, Harlan Coben, and a few other authors she wasn't familiar with. Even though she didn't share his taste in books, she liked that he was a reader. She could never understand people who weren't. To her, it was one of the greatest pleasures there was.

She was fingering the top book and thinking about how she and Chase were different yet similar when he came back into the room.

"See something you like?"

She turned around at the sound of his voice and thought, *Yes, you!* He'd changed into a pair of black cargo shorts and a white T-shirt with *Hang Loose* written in black letters, and he was still wearing his glasses.

"I prefer other genres, but these look like good choices."

He took a few steps closer. "Let me guess. You're a romance reader."

Something about the way he looked at her when he said it gave her a jolt. Or maybe it was just the word "romance" dripping off his lips. "Are you assuming that because I'm a woman?"

"There you go again, answering a question with a question. I'm telling you you'd make an excellent lawyer."

She laughed. "Fine. I do read romance, but I read other genres too."

He nodded, seemingly unsurprised by her answer. "My sister reads romance too. Loves it—pun intended."

This would have been the perfect time to tell him she was a romance writer, but she still held back, and she wasn't sure why. She didn't have time to contemplate it further because he'd turned and was heading toward the door.

"Ready to go?"

"Yes." Since she already had her purse and keys in hand, she said, "How about if I drive this time?"

"Fine by me."

When she walked over to the red Jeep, he glanced at her with surprise.

"What?" she said after they'd hopped in.

"Nothing."

"It was something."

He chuckled. "I was expecting a four-door sedan, that's all."

Her eyebrows went up, and she shot him a mock scowl. "Do I look that boring?"

He shook his head. "Not boring, just practical."

"Is that what you think of me?"

"It's not a bad thing, Callie. You have to stop thinking I'm criticizing you."

She sighed. "You're right. It's just that I do drive a four-door sedan at home."

"Oops."

She laughed. "It's okay. I get it. I come across as a no-nonsense kind of woman."

"I've learned that everyone has different sides. There's the persona we show the world, and then there's our private persona. Sometimes they're quite different."

"Is that true for you?"

When he didn't answer, she said, "You know what? Never mind. What sounds good for dinner?"

He laughed. "I figured you'd already done the research and knew what you wanted."

"I have, but I was just being polite."

"So, what will it be?"

"Brennecke's Beach Broiler. Say that five times fast!"

"I won't even attempt it, but I trust your judgment."

She'd chosen the restaurant because it was right on Poipu Beach, and after dinner, they could watch the sunset from there. A few minutes later, they pulled into the parking lot, and she shut off the car.

"I just realized I'm still wearing my glasses," Chase said and started to remove them.

"They look good on you."

"Yeah?"

She nodded. "Someone might even say sexy."

He grinned. "Someone?"

"Me, okay. Now, are you coming or not?"

She got out of the Jeep without waiting, and when he joined her, he was still wearing the glasses.

She eyed him suspiciously.

"Hey. If the lady thinks my glasses are sexy, I'm wearing them. Don't judge." Then he placed his palm on the small of her back and guided her toward the restaurant.

She tried not to read too much into it, but she liked the feel of his warm hand through her thin cotton sundress. He kept it there while the hostess led them to a table with a spectacular ocean view.

Tonight Callie was determined to keep things light and breezy. She wasn't going to try and pick his brain or bring up topics that made him uneasy. She'd simply let the evening unfold and enjoy his company.

After perusing the menu and placing their orders, she settled in and looked out at the scenery.

"I'm really going to miss this," she said wistfully.

"We still have quite a bit of time left. I didn't mean *we* as in *us*. I meant you and me separately..."

She smiled. "No worries. After our last discussion, I know exactly where we stand." She wasn't sure she sounded convincing, though.

"You came to the right place for inspiration for your novel."

She knew he meant Hawaii in general, but what he didn't know was how much inspiration he'd provided.

"You're right. Being here has helped my writing a lot."

"I'm glad. You obviously love what you do. I wish I could say the same."

He looked like he was ready to divulge some more, but then the waitress appeared with their drinks and appetizers.

After she left, Callie took a sip of her mai tai, which was the drink special of the evening. The fruity concoction mixed with rum went down smooth, and she reminded herself to go slow.

"Good stuff, huh?" he said after tasting his own drink.

He'd ordered a Poipu Kiss Martini. Thinking like a writer, she'd wondered if it was foreshadowing.

"Mm-hmm. So, tell me more about your sister." She figured that would be a neutral enough topic.

She listened closely as he related stories about his younger sibling, Miranda, and she got a real sense of how much he loved her. From there, their conversation flowed smoothly, and she told him more about her parents and Quinn, who was like a sister to her.

In between, they sipped their cocktails and ate the wonderful food while glancing out the window every so often at the magnificent view.

"Would you like another drink?" the waitress asked after a while.

She should have declined, because she was already in that happy place where all was right with the world.

"I'll take one. Callie?" Chase said.

He was still wearing his glasses, and she took one look into those green-gray eyes and crumbled. "Sure."

After the waitress walked away, she wondered if she'd end up regretting it.

Chapter 20

By the time they finished dinner, Chase was buzzing, and it wasn't just from the cocktails. It was Callie, sweet and sexy with her floral-print sundress, silky dark hair, and deep brown eyes like pools of chocolate.

Pools of chocolate? Really? You've been reading too much romance!

And he had. He'd finished the first book in her series and had purchased the second, feeling like a total wuss when he'd downloaded it on his Kindle app. But the more he read, the more he felt like he knew her. It was like he'd gotten a glimpse into her world, and he liked what he'd discovered.

On the downside, he didn't relish the thought of her inspiration coming from her ex-boyfriend. It was stupid for him to be jealous, but he was. He didn't like the idea of her doing the things she'd written about with her ex or any guy who wasn't him.

It was wrong, and he knew it, yet he couldn't seem to stop himself. They'd established that neither of them was ready for another relationship, but all he could think about lately was kissing her.

All during dinner, he'd had to stop himself from staring at her lips and remembering how it had felt to hold her in his arms. Now they were strolling down a path from the restaurant to the beach, and he shoved his hands in his shorts pockets to keep from reaching for her.

It didn't help that they were surrounded by couples holding hands or arm in arm as they joined the exodus to the beach. Once they reached the sand, they paused to remove their shoes, and he offered his arm so she could steady herself as she slipped off her sandals.

By silent agreement, they walked until they'd reached a stretch of sand away from the masses. Callie immediately dug her phone out of her purse and began snapping pictures. Chase thought about doing the same, but he wanted to keep his hands free in case...

"Isn't this spectacular?" she breathed.

"It is."

The descending sun painted the sky in brilliant yellows, oranges, and reds. The waves lapped rhythmically against the shore, and the wind whistled through the palm trees. There were murmurs from the other spectators, but their voices were low and respectful, almost like they were in church. It really was a spectacular scene, but he was distracted by the beautiful woman beside him, who was moving around and snapping pictures from different angles.

At one point, she stepped in front of him to capture a certain shot, and he placed his hands on her waist to keep her steady. Plus, it was an excuse to touch her.

She glanced over her shoulder, her eyes bright and smile wide. "Hey. Would you mind taking a picture with me?"

"Sure. Why not?"

He expected her to break out of his hold and stand beside him, but instead, she stepped back so her backside was flush with his front and held the phone up in the air. She shifted around, trying to find the best angle, her dress brushing against his bare legs and making him squirm.

"Here. Let me hold the phone since my arms are longer," he suggested.

She handed it to him, leaned back, and rested her head on his shoulder while he took over. He could have stayed like that all night, but eventually he'd have to snap the photo.

With one arm looped around her waist, he held her close. "Ready? Look up and smile."

They tilted their heads up and smiled, and he hit the button a few times.

Instead of moving away, Callie said, "Let's check and make sure they're good."

He kept his arm around her while they previewed the pictures he'd taken. He thought they were all good, but she didn't seem completely satisfied.

"Let's take a couple more," she said.

"We could walk down the beach a little further and pose on those rocks," he said, pointing to the left. Not that he was trying to take advantage of the situation, but it had been her idea to take pictures in the first place.

"Okay."

He took her hand as they headed toward an outcropping of rocks. The sun had sunk further now, and its rays spread out on the horizon in a dazzling display. There were only a few more minutes of daylight left, so he picked up his pace.

Callie held his hand tightly and matched her steps to his.

Once they reached the rocks, he let go. "I'll get into position and then give you a hand up."

"Be careful. They might be slippery," she said.

Some of the rocks were dry on top where the waves hadn't wetted them, and Chase picked his way along until he found one with a wide, flat top that was mostly dry. "Found one. Give me your hand."

She slipped her hand into his again, and he noted her willingness to trust him as he pulled her up onto the rock. She wobbled a bit and brushed up against him, and then they were facing each other.

In that moment, time stopped, and Chase forgot why they were even there. He gazed down at her, backlit by the sunset, her hair brushing her bare shoulders, and he lost all ability to think. He only wanted to feel.

Callie hadn't budged, and her eyes locked on his, searching them, for what, he wasn't sure. Did she want him to back away or come closer? Her lips parted, and her chest rose and fell, but was it from the exertion of climbing on the rocks or from being so close? He felt completely inept standing there, and he waited for a sign.

Just then a wave crashed against the rocks and splashed them, but Callie got the brunt of it since she was partially blocking him. She gave a little cry and fell against him, wrapping her arms around his waist to gain hold.

It was as if Mother Nature was trying to push them together again. This time, when he looked down at her, there was no mistaking the invitation in her beautiful brown eyes.

He slowly dipped his head down, giving her a chance to back away, but if anything, she pressed her body closer. His hands went around her waist and locked her in place, and he lowered his lips to hers.

He'd intended on going slow, but Callie opened her mouth to him, and their kiss ignited. He felt ravenous as he plundered her mouth and tangled with her tongue. He tasted the fruitiness of her cocktail and smelled the sweet scent of her perfume as she tucked her body around him, surrendering completely and giving as much as she took.

Her breasts were smashed against him, and his erection pressed into her stomach. He couldn't be sure how long they kissed, but when she pulled back, he decided it wasn't nearly long enough.

"Chase?" They were both panting and staring at each other with surprise and longing.

He brushed her hair off her shoulder and braced himself for whatever came next.

"Let's go home."

Chapter 21

Callie was shaking as they drove back to the resort, and she clamped her hands on the wheel to stop the tremors. Kissing Chase hadn't been part of the plan, but now that she had...

He kept shooting her concerned glances, and she knew she should say something, but she wasn't sure what. Every nerve ending tingled, and her body sizzled with awareness of him.

She felt unbearably warm, so she rolled down her window, but just as quickly, she got chilled and rolled it back up again. A couple of times, Chase opened his mouth to speak, but then he'd snap it shut again.

Luckily, it was a short ride, and Callie couldn't wait to park and escape the confined space. She'd think better once there was some distance between them. They walked up to their front doors in awkward silence and then paused.

"Callie, I..."

"No. You don't have to say anything."

"But..."

"I'm not angry at you."

He looked visibly relieved and let out a sigh. He took a step closer, and she sucked in a breath. She was afraid that if he came too close, she'd yank him into her condo and rip his clothes off.

Seeming to sense her hesitation, he halted, but he reached out and fixed the strap of her dress, that had slipped down her shoulder. The pads of his fingertips brushed her bare skin and made her tingly all over again.

"Callie."

"We said we weren't doing this."

"Doing what?"

"Getting involved."

"We just kissed. It's not like we signed a contract or anything."

"I know, but it could lead to more kissing, which might lead to..."

"Having sex."

He phrased it like a statement of fact rather than a question, and her stomach flipped. She hadn't expected him to be so direct, since he seldom ever was. But his confidence was showing, and he grinned. "We're adults, Callie. I'm just telling it like it is."

"Is that...is that what you want?"

"Do you?"

"Here we go again."

He chuckled and closed the distance between them. He hesitated as if waiting for her to stop him, but she couldn't. Slipping his arms around her waist, he said, "I want whatever you want."

Her heart was pounding out of her chest, and her nipples were trying to poke holes through her dress. Placing his index finger under her chin, he tipped her face up and searched her eyes. "What do you want?"

She swallowed hard while wriggling a little closer. "I'll take another kiss."

"Should we step inside for this one?"

"I'm not sure it's safe."

He chuckled and then lightly brushed her lips with his. "Why not?"

"I'm afraid we might not come back out."

His eyes blazed. "I'm willing to risk it whenever you are."

Her brain felt like it was short-circuiting. There was too much conflicting data to make a rational decision. If she were a different type of person, she'd have dragged him into her condo by now, consequences be damned. But she wasn't experienced with casual encounters. She'd had one long-term relationship, and she'd been absent from the dating scene for what felt like ages. Besides, this wasn't supposed to happen. Not here. Not now.

"You just talked yourself out of it, didn't you?"

He spoke softly with a hint of disappointment. She had to give him credit for his patience and for allowing her to set the course of their "relationship."

Sliding her hands up his arms, she clasped them behind his neck. "I'm sorry."

"It's okay. I get it."

For two people who'd just agreed they weren't having sex, they certainly weren't in any hurry to say goodnight.

"I had a great time."

"Me too."

"Thanks for watching the sunset with me."

"Thanks for kissing me."

Her heart fluttered. "You're a good kisser."

"So are you."

"For the record, I was this close to saying yes." She removed her arms from around his neck and brought her thumb and forefinger together as close as they could go without touching.

"For the record, I really wanted you to. But I totally understand why you didn't."

"Care to explain it to me, then?" She placed her hands on his shoulders, enjoying the feel of his warm, hard muscles beneath her fingertips.

"You're not a 'casual fling' kind of woman, and you don't play games. When you're interested in someone, you're all in and loyal almost to a fault."

She bristled at that, remembering what had happened with Adam. She'd been so trusting and secure in their love that she hadn't even considered the possibility of him cheating.

"Am I right?"

It was almost like he knew her intimately, even though they hadn't known each other that long.

"Am I that easy to read?"

"Here we go again," he said, laughing.

She sighed and leaned her forehead against his chest. "Sometimes I wish I were different. I wish I were more spontaneous and adventurous."

"Hey," he said, pulling her tighter against his hard chest. "Don't beat yourself up. I happen to think you're pretty perfect just the way you are."

Tipping her head up, she said, "You're not just saying that to get me to change my mind, are you?"

He laughed louder this time. "If I were trying to do that, I'd be showing rather than telling, if you know what I mean."

"Showing?"

Cupping her face in his hands, he dipped his head down and kissed her. Just like at the beach, the kiss quickly intensified, and she welcomed his tongue like a long-lost friend. His hands slid down her bare arms and snaked around her back. In a surprise move, he cupped her butt cheeks and pulled her hips forward. This time, there was no mistaking his arousal, and it fueled her own.

But after a few minutes, the beam of a car's headlights shone on them and broke them out of their lusty trance. They quickly parted, realizing they'd been putting on a show for any passersby to see. Plus, they'd been illuminated by the lampposts that came on automatically in front of every unit.

Callie felt both irritated and grateful for the interruption.

Rubbing the back of his neck with one hand, Chase was already fitting his key into the lock with the other. "We should get inside," he said almost apologetically.

She nodded, agreeing it was for the best.

"Good night, Callie."

"Good night."

Once she'd gone inside, she slumped down on the couch and silently berated herself for not going through with it. He'd called them adults, but she certainly didn't feel like one. Why had she turned him down? What would have been wrong with a casual hook-up? It might have been the best thing for her—another step toward healing after Adam's betrayal and her grandma's death.

It wasn't like Chase was a stranger she'd picked up at a bar. She knew him (somewhat) and liked him, and so far, he'd been the perfect gentleman. He'd also been completely honest about his intentions, so she knew where he stood. There'd be no false hopes about where this would lead or if they would continue to see each other after they returned to Michigan.

If they got together, it would be a sweet escape, a fun vacation memory. Coming to Hawaii had motivated her to start writing again, and maybe being with Chase would give her renewed confidence when it came to men and dating.

In effect, Chase would be helping her in two ways—with her writing and rejuvenating her spirits. Truthfully, he was already doing that, but being intimate with him would take it to a whole other level.

Just imagine the book material you'd have then!

Chapter 22

Chase went for a morning run even though he'd slept horribly the night before. He'd lain in bed for hours, tossing and turning and thinking about kissing Callie. He'd kept listening for sounds from her unit, hoping she might change her mind and knock on his door, but all he'd heard was the loud ticking of the clock, and as the hours had passed, he'd realized she wouldn't be knocking.

He'd resorted to self-pleasure, but it hadn't been satisfying, and afterward, he'd lain there wondering what it would have been like had she said yes. Would she be like the heroines in her books—passionate and responsive? He'd guess yes based on the way she'd kissed him. She hadn't held back at all. She'd pressed herself against him and matched his energy and enthusiasm with every kiss. She'd probably be the same way in bed, although he might never get the opportunity to find out.

While he'd been frustrated, he hadn't been angry. In fact, he respected her for knowing herself and sticking to her guns. But he already despised the next guy who'd come along and be lucky enough to experience all the fire and passion that was inside of her.

He understood she'd been hurt by her ex and was being cautious, but he couldn't imagine her staying single for long. She had too much to offer, and it was just a matter of time before she'd meet someone and fall in love again.

On the other hand, he was still a cynical SOB and couldn't see himself going down that path again. He would have been all for a vacation fling if she'd been willing, but that wasn't what she wanted. So, while he'd like to spend more time with her, he'd need to keep his fantasies to himself. If she wanted more kissing, he'd be happy to oblige, but he couldn't expect it to go any further.

On the way back from his run, he glanced up at her unit, but her blinds were still closed. He wondered if she were sleeping in or had gone somewhere. Since it was mid-morning, there was also the possibility that she was busy writing and hadn't bothered to open the curtains yet.

It was another gorgeous day, but he guessed she'd try to keep her distance, and he had no choice but to let her. However, if he happened to run into her around the resort, who knew what might happen.

He went inside, took a shower, and thought about what he could do today. After he got dressed, though, he realized he was still tired from the night before. He decided to take his book—his physical book, not his phone with the Kindle app—and sit outside and read for a while. He might even try taking a much-needed nap.

But just after he'd collected his book, a towel, and his sunglasses, his phone rang. He should have known.

"Hey, sis."

"Did you kiss her yet?"

"Who?" He knew exactly who she was referring to, but he couldn't resist teasing her.

"You know who! Callie Cooper. My favorite romance author ever!"

Chase rolled his eyes at that and slumped down on the couch. "If I answer you, what's in it for me?"

"Never-ending love and affection?"

"You're supposed to give that to me anyway."

"Dinner out when you get back home?"

"Are we talking McDonald's or something better?"

"Whatever you want within reason. I'm on a budget, you know."

"Fine. And the answer is yes."

She literally screamed in his ear, and he held the phone away until she'd finished.

"Seriously? She might have heard that through the wall."

"Sorry. I just can't believe you kissed someone famous."

"Famous?" He'd never thought of Callie that way, and he doubted she did either. She was way too humble for that.

"She's not J.K. Rowling, Miranda."

"I know, but she's well known in the romance world. Have you seen how many followers she has on Facebook? Thousands!"

He chuckled. "That's all fine and good, but here she's just Callie. I don't think anyone has recognized her." And she probably preferred it that way. She was someone who liked to blend in, not draw attention to herself.

"Well, I would if I saw her. Speaking of which…"

He could practically see her wheels spinning. "No, Miranda."

"You don't even know what I was going to say."

"I have a pretty good guess. You're thinking of coming here to meet her."

"I'd be coming to visit my big brother, and it's Hawaii. Hello!"

"I can't let you come here."

"What? You can't stop me."

"You'll ruin everything. Callie still doesn't know that I know who she is. It's better this way, believe me."

"That's ridiculous. Why wouldn't an author want to meet one of their biggest fans?"

"Under different circumstances, I'm sure she'd be flattered, but she came here to relax, not be fawned over by some overzealous fan."

"Overzealous? Wow. Big word. You've been reading."

He sighed. "Listen to me. My relationship with Callie is…tricky."

"What do you mean? What did you do to her?"

"Nothing. We kissed, but that was all."

"You don't sound very happy about it."

"The kissing was great, but Callie and I agreed we don't want to get involved. We're only here for a while, and we might never see each other again." He didn't dare tell his sister where Callie lived lest she scream in his ear again. But as an avid fan, he wondered if she already knew. Did authors share things like that? He hadn't looked at her Facebook page, but now that Miranda had brought it up, he was curious.

"She lives in Michigan, you know. I don't know where exactly, but based on some of her posts, I think it might be in the metro Detroit area. Wouldn't that be awesome if she lives close by?"

"Yeah. Awesome." There was his answer. Miranda probably knew almost as much about Callie as he did.

"I gotta go, but I'm not giving up on the idea of coming to visit you."

"Miranda…"

"I'll give you a little bit more time to get to know her. But what's wrong with you? Ramp up your game. I would love to have Callie Cooper as my sister-in-law."

"That's it. You gotta go, and so do I."

"Love you."

"Love you too."

After he hung up, he sat there staring at the phone and shaking his head. The last thing he needed was his sister to show up and blow it for him. He suspected Callie wouldn't take kindly to finding out that he'd known about her career for some time and hadn't told her. Knowing her, she'd probably wonder what else he'd been keeping from her, and keeping secrets wasn't a solid start to a relationship.

Wait a minute. Relationship? They weren't even supposed to have a *relationship*. But what should he call it, then? He was so confused.

"This is exactly why I shouldn't get involved." But it was too late. He already was.

Chapter 23

Callie was writing the first sex scene in her new novel, which was often a daunting task. She'd always spent more time on those scenes because she wanted to get them just right. She strived to place the focus on the emotions between the characters rather than the mechanics of the act, and she was careful with her word choices.

When she'd written her first romance novel, she'd been very aware that her grandmother and mother would likely be her first readers. She'd even thought ahead to when she had children someday. All of that had helped shape her writing, and as a result, her books were what she'd call sweet with a touch of heat.

She smiled remembering her grandma's reaction after reading her first book. "Whew! I had to break out my fan during that first sex scene between Jason and Samantha!" Irene had said with a smile.

"Was it too much?" Callie asked worriedly.

"No. It was perfect. I loved it," Irene replied.

"You're not just saying that because I'm your granddaughter, are you?"

"Have you ever known me to sugarcoat things?"

"Well, no…"

"I'm telling you the truth, dear. I loved the story, and you captured the passion between the characters perfectly."

Callie had beamed with pride because her grandma's opinion had been hugely important to her. Irene had always been an avid romance reader, and if she thought the book was good, Callie hoped other fans of the genre would too.

Her mom's reaction had been slightly different. "Well. I have to say it was a little strange reading a love scene written by my daughter. But after a while, I kind of forgot it was your writing and got lost in the story."

"But was it good? Did you like it?"

"It was very good. It grabbed my attention right away and didn't let go until the last page. But I'm not sure your father should read it."

Callie laughed. "I wouldn't ask him to."

"But he wants to support your career."

"He can support me in other ways."

And he had. Whenever she'd released a new book, her father would take some copies to work with him.

He'd hand them out to anyone who was interested and then ask them to write reviews for her.

Quinn had done the same thing, and Callie credited them both for jump-starting her career. It hadn't been easy, and at times, she'd almost given up, but now she was glad she hadn't. She had over ten novels to her name and a solid fan base that was growing every day. Sometimes she still couldn't believe it, but she loved what she did, and it was finally paying off. If only Irene were there to enjoy it with her.

Just then, movement outside caught her eye, and she glanced up from the dining room table where she'd been writing.

It was Chase, dragging a lounge chair from his patio onto the lawn. She ducked down so he couldn't see her and watched him go back into his unit and then return with a towel and a book. He laid the towel on the chair, sat down, and immediately opened his book.

He'd angled the chair toward the sun, which gave her a view of his profile, and she sighed. He must not have shaved, because she saw the distinct outline of stubble on his jaw. She wondered what it would feel like against her face. He ran a hand through his hair, and she remembered sliding her fingertips into it the other night. He held up his book to block the sun, and she saw his arm muscles tighten, just like they had when he'd hooked them around her waist and drawn her close.

She shifted in her chair, the memory of his kisses stirring her libido all over again. She considered going outside to say hello, but she still felt embarrassed about turning him down. She'd planned on taking a few days to cool off, but apparently, that wasn't going to happen.

She turned back to her laptop and continued writing her scene, but she kept getting distracted anytime Chase moved. She closed her eyes and breathed deeply, trying to refocus her brain on the task at hand. But when she reopened them, another movement caught her attention.

Chase was standing next to the lounge chair and had just whipped off his white T-shirt. He stood with his back to her, his hands on his hips as he looked out at the ocean. Her eyes wandered down his back to the waistband of his shorts, where those sexy indents were. His butt was high and round, his legs long and lean. Talk about inspiring. But her concentration had vanished, and she stood up, deciding to go outside and talk to him.

Then a woman came into view, wearing a red bikini and flip-flops and carrying a striped beach bag. Callie watched Chase turn to look at the woman, and she wondered if he'd gotten whiplash. She could hardly blame him, though. The woman's bikini was like a siren call, which, Callie supposed, was the intention. She'd been heading toward the pool, and when she glanced over and saw Chase looking, she smiled and waved.

Tramp.

Chase hesitated for a second, almost as if he wasn't sure she was waving at him, and then he held up his hand and waved back.

Keep walking. Keep walking. Wrong way. Wrong way!

The woman veered off the cement path and strode across the lawn toward Chase, quickly closing the distance between them with her long, slender legs.

Figures. Am I the only short woman around here?

It was like driving past the scene of an accident; Callie couldn't look away. And in this case, she stared hard, knowing neither of them could see her behind the curtain. Well, they probably could have if they'd bothered looking, but they were only looking at each other.

If only my windows were open so I could hear what they're saying. Then again, maybe I'd rather not.

The woman set down her beach bag and treated Chase to an unobstructed view of her bikini body. She extended her arm, which was layered with gold bangles that shone in the sunlight.

Seriously? Who wears that much jewelry to the pool? It's very impractical.

Chase shook her hand enthusiastically (at least, that's how Callie perceived it), and it seemed to last longer than was absolutely necessary for a first meeting.

Terrific! I turned him down, and now Siren shows up with her boobs hanging out. In all fairness, they weren't hanging out. They were sitting up high and perky, and Callie questioned if they were real. Siren had white blonde hair that she wore in a swingy ponytail, and she looked to be about twenty-five, tops.

Jealousy aside, she was quite pretty in a beachy, California-girl way. In other words, she was exactly the opposite of Callie. How ironic that Callie had been born in California, yet her name was the only thing she had to show for it. Callie's mother was Italian, and her father was a mix of English and German, but Callie had inherited her mother's dark hair and eyes and, unfortunately, her diminutive stature.

Normally, she embraced her heritage, but today she wished she'd had a few more inches on her—in height and boob size. *Oh well.*

Chase was talking now, and he was waving his hands around like he was the Italian. Then he pointed toward the cliff that he'd jumped from, and Callie nodded along, like she knew exactly what he was saying. He was probably regaling the woman with the story of his heroic jump, and she was captivated by his every word.

The woman turned in the direction he was pointing, giving Chase and Callie a view of her backside. Her bikini made Callie's look like a romper. The bottoms were held up by strings hastily tied at her narrow hips, and the back rode up to show most of her butt cheeks and the tan lines they were supposed to be covering.

Callie shook her head in disgust. This woman knew exactly what she was doing, and Chase appeared to be a willing participant. The next thing she knew, he grabbed his towel off the chair, abandoning his T-shirt and book, and the two of them started walking away down the path.

"No, no, no!" Callie whisper-hissed. "You're going the wrong way." Not to mention that he'd carelessly left his book lying in the hot sun. Didn't he realize the cover might get warped?

But they were walking purposefully toward the beach, and soon she wouldn't be able to see them. Callie was horrified, and not just at them, but at herself for feeling crazed with jealousy.

Chase wasn't hers to feel jealous over. She'd had her chance with him, and she'd blown it. She'd thought so last night, but now she knew so. If they'd slept together, she felt certain this wouldn't be happening right now. Like he'd said, he was a one-woman man, and she could have been that woman. Instead, he was strolling down the path with a stranger in a red bikini that screamed, "Take me. I'm yours!"

"What should I do? What should I do?" She looked around the room like somebody might answer and then threw her hands in the air.

Quinn wasn't there, but she heard her voice clear as day: "Go after him."

Callie didn't hesitate. She ran into the bedroom and pulled out her floral print bikini, the one she'd worn when she'd gone to the beach with Chase. It wouldn't give her an advantage over the competition, but it was better than the alternative, the dreaded black one-piece.

She hurriedly tugged it on, though why did it seem tighter than the last time she'd worn it? Then she grabbed her beach bag and sunglasses and went to the patio door, where she hurriedly donned her flip-flops. She didn't bother locking up, because Hawaii was too mellow for burglaries, right? Stupid logic, but she didn't have time to overthink it.

Instead, she started down the path toward the beach, wondering what on earth she was going to do once she got there.

Chapter 24

Chase felt guilty, but he shouldn't have. It's not like he and Callie had a "thing." They'd kissed a few times, but she'd made it clear that was as far as it would go. So why should he feel guilty about walking along the beach with Sara of the red bikini? She seemed like a nice enough girl, although rather on the young side, twenty-five to be exact. When she'd come up and introduced herself, he'd had no intentions other than being polite. But then she'd mentioned wanting to jump off the cliff, and when he'd told her he'd done it, she asked if he'd go with her.

"Are you here alone?" he asked, making conversation as they climbed the trail to the clifftop.

"No. I'm with my parents, but they would never do something like this. I'm glad I ran into you."

He wasn't sure how to respond because he had a feeling he might regret this. Not jumping, but agreeing to accompany her. She'd looked up at him with starry eyes, and he didn't want her to get the wrong idea. He wasn't about to become a play toy for a bored twenty-five-year-old woman on vacation. He could practically hear Eric yelling, "You wuss!" but he tried to ignore it.

Once they reached the top of the cliff, they lined up behind a handful of other brave souls and waited their turn.

"What about you? Are you here with someone?" Sara asked.

"No. I'm on sabbatical."

"Are you a doctor?"

"A lawyer."

"Hmm."

He wasn't sure if she was impressed or not, but it didn't matter. This might be the first and last time he'd ever see her.

He glanced out over the ocean and took in the beautiful sight. He'd already been there a while, but the view never got old. He scanned the horizon and then looked down to the beach.

Wait a minute. Is that? Yes, it is her. He spotted Callie down below, spreading her towel out on the sand not too far from where he and Sara had set their things.

He shouldn't have been surprised to see her there, but he was. He figured she'd be holed up in her condo, writing until at least dinnertime. In a few short weeks, he'd already become accustomed to her patterns. Crazy.

He might not have noticed her but for the methodical way she went about laying out the towel and making sure to secure the ends with items from her oversized beach bag. For some reason, he smiled as he watched her.

"Chase?"

He brought his attention back to Sara. "Yeah?"

"I just asked where you're from?"

"Oh. Michigan."

"Brrr."

He chuckled. "What about you?"

"San Diego."

He'd have guessed as much, but he wasn't up for small talk. He was more interested in what Callie was doing, although several of the younger guys waiting to jump had cast him envious glances.

There was no doubt that Sara was eye-catching, but so was Callie, though in a different way. Her beauty was subtler, and she often tried to hide it, unlike Sara, Kelsey, and Tina, who enjoyed flaunting theirs. If he were younger, those three women would have held more appeal, but as it was, Callie had them all beat.

As the line moved forward, he got an even better view of her, and now she was rubbing on sunscreen thoroughly and in the same order as last time. A few times, she glanced up to the clifftop, and he thought she might have spotted him, but he couldn't be sure.

If she had, she'd probably noticed Sara, who was standing even closer to him now that it was almost their turn to jump. Some people jumped in pairs, holding hands and screeching with fear and excitement before they splashed into the water below.

Up until then, Sara hadn't shown any signs of fear, but now she looked up at him warily and said, "Will you jump with me?"

"Um..."

"Please?"

Chase caught eyes with the guy standing behind them, who scowled at him like he couldn't believe Chase had even hesitated. The stranger wouldn't have a clue that Chase was worrying about Callie seeing him with Sara. He reminded himself that he was being ridiculous and wasn't doing anything wrong.

"Sure," he finally said.

Sara looked relieved and leaned into his side, accidentally (or not) rubbing her boob against his arm.

It had been impossible not to notice them given the way they were showcased in her tiny bikini top. He wondered if she was worried about losing her swimsuit when they jumped, but he didn't have time to ask.

"You two are up," said the scowling guy behind them.

"Ready?" Chase asked her.

She nodded, but she didn't look nearly as brave as she had when they'd first discussed this.

"On the count of three." He took her left hand and clasped it tightly. "One, two, three!"

Then they were airborne, tucking into a ball and Sara plugging her nose with her free hand, her ponytail flying straight up in the air. It was over quickly, and they hit the water with a loud splash before reemerging to cheers from the clifftop and the beach.

He'd let go of her hand once they'd landed, and now she reached for it again as they trudged up to shore. Chase felt obligated to help her out of the water due to the strong undertow. He tightly clasped her hand while seeking out Callie, hoping she wasn't looking.

No such luck. She was sitting up on her towel with her arms hugging her knees and looking straight at them. At least, he assumed so. He couldn't see her eyes behind her sunglasses, but her head was turned in their direction.

Once he and Sara got to shore, he let go of her hand again, and she gave him a confused look.

"I see someone I know. I'm going over to say hello."

"Oh. Okay," she said disappointedly.

"I'll rejoin you in a minute." He really didn't want to, though. Now that Callie was there, he'd rather sit and talk with her, but that would be rude to Sara. *Here's more evidence that women are trouble. If you'd have kept to yourself, you wouldn't be in this awkward position.*

He and Sara split off, and he walked toward Callie, who'd turned her head the opposite way as if she hadn't wanted him to see her.

"Hey."

"Hello," she replied icily.

"How are you?" His heart was knocking around in his chest, and he shifted uncomfortably. *Is she pissed at me?*

"Fine. How are you?"

He hated their stilted attempt at conversation, yet he wasn't ready to walk away. "I just jumped again. Not sure if you saw me…"

"I saw you."

There was no mistaking the chill in her tone. But why should he apologize for whatever it was she was silently accusing him of? *Women are so damned confusing.*

"Her name is Sara. The woman I jumped with."

"Um-hmm."

"She introduced herself to me in front of my unit."

"Oh?"

"We started talking about cliff jumping, and she said she'd been wanting to try it."

"So, naturally, you volunteered to go with her."

"Are you pissed?"

"Why should I be?"

"Here we go again." This time, neither of them laughed.

"What you do and with whom is your business."

"True."

"Well, have fun with Sandra."

"Sara." He got the impression she'd said the name wrong on purpose, and he almost chuckled, but he didn't dare. Callie might be petite, but she was a force to be reckoned with.

"I don't plan on spending all day with her," he added.

"Just long enough, then?"

Ouch. "I was just being friendly."

"Friend away. Don't let me stop you." She flapped her hand around as if dismissing him, but he stood his ground.

"What about you?"

"What about me?"

"I'd have jumped with you too if you'd asked me. In fact, I'd rather it had been you." That got her attention.

She snapped her head up, slid her sunglasses down her nose, and studied him. "Are you serious, or are you just saying that because you don't think I'd do it?"

"Would you?"

"Here we go again." This time she laughed, and it warmed him to the bones.

"I'll go with you right now if you want to."

"What about Sandra?"

"Sara."

"Whatever."

"She'll be fine, and I doubt she'll be alone for long."

Callie narrowed her eyes at him, and he realized his mistake. "I had no ill intentions toward her. She wanted a jumping partner, and I was just being…"

"Friendly. Yeah, you said that."

"Look, Callie…"

But he didn't finish because she suddenly stood up. "Let's do it."

"Huh?" He wasn't sure how to take that sentence, but he had a few good ideas.

"Jump. Let's jump together."

"Are you sure?"

"You don't believe me."

"I didn't say that."

"But you were thinking it. I can tell."

"So, you think you know me that well?" he teased.

"I know *some* things about you." She tilted her pretty head and smiled up at him. *Is she flirting with me? No. Can't be.*

"Okay, then. Let's do this." He almost took her hand, but then he realized Sara was expecting him to return, and he didn't want to look like a two-timing douchebag.

While Callie was leaning over and stuffing things back into her beach bag for safekeeping, he glanced over to where he'd left his things. Sure enough, some guy had already sat down next to Sara, and Chase was relieved.

It looked like the young ripped guy who'd been standing in line behind them on the cliff. Figured. But Chase could have hugged the guy because now he could concentrate on Callie, which was where his mind had been all along.

They trudged through the sand to the trail, and as they neared Sara, Callie said, "Do you want to stop and say something to her?"

This woman never ceased to amaze him. Even though she'd obviously been jealous, she couldn't help being polite. It was in her nature, and it was one more thing he admired about her.

"She looks pretty busy," he replied watching the muscle-bound guy lean in and say something that made Sara laugh. Sara glanced up at Chase and Callie as they came closer, but she just nodded and went back to talking to her new friend.

"I guess you're right," Callie said.

Once they reached the beginning of the trail, he paused and turned to look at her. "You don't have to do this, you know? You don't have to prove anything to me."

She punched her hands on her hips, and said, "I'm doing this, and you can't stop me."

He laughed, loving when she got sassy with him.

"Okay, then. Let's go."

He took her hand to help her up the path, but really, he just wanted an excuse to touch her. She didn't pull back and he was grateful.

He felt like they were starting over or picking up from where they'd left off. He wasn't sure which, but it felt damn good.

Chapter 25

Callie couldn't believe she'd done it. "That was amazing!" she said as she and Chase walked up the beach together. Sara and the muscly guy were gone, but Chase didn't comment on it. He was completely focused on her, and she had to admit it felt damn good!

"Aren't you glad you did it?"

"So glad. If only I had a video to prove it. Nobody at home will believe me."

He chuckled. "I'll vouch for you."

She shot him a glance. Had he realized what he'd just said? Did he plan on staying in touch after they returned to Michigan?

"We should celebrate tonight." *Whoa, girl. Jumping off a cliff doesn't have to be a metaphor for your life.*

"Really?" He glanced down at her, surprised.

"Just because we didn't sleep together doesn't mean I don't like hanging out with you."

"I like hanging out with you too," he said, his eyes crinkling at the corners.

Thank goodness they were back to normal again. She'd hated seeing him with Sara. She'd felt like she'd lost him, though he wasn't hers to lose. She kept having to remind herself of that, but it was getting more difficult by the day.

"Where are you taking me to dinner?" he said.

"My place?"

He came to a dead stop in the middle of the path. "You sure about that?"

"I'm a good cook if that's what you're worried about."

"That's not what I'm worried about, and you know it."

She looked into his gorgeous green-gray eyes and swallowed hard. She knew exactly what he was referring to. "Are you afraid of me?"

He slowly shook his head. "Hell no."

"Then come over and have dinner."

He hesitated for a few seconds and then said, "Okay."

She put on a brave smile. "Good. I'll need time to change and prepare a few things."

"No problem. I need a shower anyway."

Chase in the shower, dripping wet...mmm...

"Can I bring anything?"

Just your gorgeous self. "I think I have everything I need."

"What about wine?"

"Except that."

"I'll bring the wine, then."

"Great."

They walked the rest of the way in silence, but her mind was reeling. Had she really just invited him to her place? Talk about tempting fate. But it was too late to retract the invitation, and truthfully, she liked the idea of cooking for him. She hadn't cooked much at all since being on the island, and a homemade meal sounded like a refreshing change.

"What time do you want me?" he asked once they'd reached their patios.

Oh God. I'm never going to survive tonight. "Six o'clock okay?"

"Works for me."

She nodded and wondered if he was as nervous as she was.

"See you in a little while," he said.

Once she was inside her place, she let out a huge sigh and then clamped her hand over her mouth. She hadn't heard much through the walls, but just in case.

She waited until she was in her bedroom with the door closed to start talking out loud. "Stop freaking out. You can do this. You just jumped off a cliff, for Pete's sake!"

She started undressing and became frustrated. "Why is it so hard to get out of a wet bathing suit?" Finally, she peeled it off and went into the bathroom to hang it up to dry. When she turned around, she caught sight of her naked self in the mirror and paused.

She pinched her abdomen, thinking she might have gained a pound or two since coming there, but it wasn't a significant change, especially since she'd lost ten pounds after her break-up with Adam and Irene's death. She'd regained her appetite, and she should be happy about that.

But she also hadn't expected to get naked with someone anytime soon, so she was being extra critical. She raised her eyebrows in surprise. "You're really thinking about it, aren't you?" She answered her own question with a nod. "Ohmigod. Now I'm freaking out again."

But she was running out of time for it. She had a lot to do to prepare for Chase's arrival. First things first, she needed a shower. She turned on the water and let it warm up while she padded out to the bedroom closet. She'd been saving one dress for a special occasion. When she'd packed it, she couldn't have known what that occasion would be, but now she pulled it out of the closet.

She'd bought it when she and Quinn had gone shopping before her trip. Quinn was the one who'd found it and insisted she try it on. She'd loved it immediately, and now she was glad she'd packed it.

The dress was a sleeveless V-neck in a bright floral print that was flashier than what she usually wore. It nipped in at the waist and flared over her hips, stopping at mid-thigh. She recalled the saleswoman stating that it was made with short women in mind, and Callie had scowled at her. "I meant petite. Sorry," the woman had said before she'd slunk off. After she'd walked away, Callie and Quinn had shared a good laugh over it.

She laid the dress on the bed and pulled out the strappy sandals she'd bought to go with it. At the time, she'd asked Quinn why she even needed a dressy outfit since she'd be traveling alone. Quinn had replied, "Trust me. You never know when you might meet the man of your dreams."

The man of her dreams. She'd begun to think that there was no such thing except in fiction. That was one of the things she loved about writing and reading romance novels—their optimism. She'd been lacking that in her life lately, but she was starting to feel a flicker of it again. Was that because of Chase?

She went through her getting-ready routine like usual, and when she'd finished dressing, she surveyed herself again. She loved the dress, and on a whim, she took a selfie and sent it to Quinn with the caption: *You have great taste!*

She didn't expect a reply, because, with the time difference, Quinn would be at work, but a minute later, her phone rang, and it was Quinn.

"Ohmigod. Does this mean what I think it means?" she said excitedly.

"Meaning?"

"Are you going out with your sexy neighbor again?"

"Actually, he's coming over for dinner. I'm cooking."

"You're wearing the dress *inside*? That can only mean one thing…"

"Quinn."

"Tonight's the night, isn't it? You're going to seduce him."

Callie laughed because the thought of her seducing Chase sounded backwards. It had a nice ring to it, though. "I just felt like dressing up, Quinn. What's wrong with that?"

"Nothing. You look fab! But you could at least admit that you're considering it."

Callie sighed because she couldn't keep anything from her best friend. "Okay, fine. I'm considering it, but I have to go. He'll be here soon."

"I'm so excited for you! Have fun tonight!"

"I will. Love you."

"Love you too. Bye."

Quinn meant well, but talking to her had escalated Callie's nervousness. Giving voice to what might happen tonight made it more real. She considered changing into something more casual and less "I want to have sex with you," but then she glanced at her watch and realized she didn't have time to change. She hurried into the kitchen and started taking out ingredients from the fridge.

She would be making a chicken and vegetable stir-fry that wasn't too labor intensive. She also had a bag of rolls and a small chocolate cake for dessert. She'd planned on making the meal that night anyway, but now she'd have company—company in the form of her very handsome neighbor who'd jumped off a cliff with her and seemed prepared to do it again (figuratively speaking).

At least, that was what it felt like. She hadn't put herself out there since Adam, and that seemed like eons ago. She recalled Chase describing her as someone "who didn't do casual flings," and he'd been right. She was considering it now with him, though.

She took a few deep breaths and gave herself another pep talk.

You don't have to do anything you don't want to do. You're in charge here. It'll be fine either way. Just have fun and go with the flow.

The problem was, "going with the flow" wasn't her usual M.O. But maybe things were changing. Maybe she was changing. And change was good, right?

Chapter 26

Chase smelled something cooking as soon as he stepped out of his unit. His stomach rumbled, but he wasn't sure if it was from hunger or nerves. He'd been battling them since Callie had invited him to dinner, and he wasn't sure why. It was just dinner, right? At least, that's what he kept telling himself as he'd taken a shower, shaved, and dressed in his best polo shirt and khaki shorts.

It had taken him a ridiculous amount of time to decide what to wear and whether to spritz on cologne. He'd considered calling his sister for advice but thought better of it. She'd probably freak out if she knew he was going to Callie's place for dinner, and he was freaking out enough already.

He couldn't remember the last time he'd felt like this over a woman. Honestly, he couldn't recall ever being nervous with Cassandra. The thought nagged at him until he finally came up with the reason. Cass had been a sure thing—the way she'd looked at him, flirted with him, and stood close when they were talking. She'd displayed interest in him from the start, and that had given him the confidence to ask her out.

The situation with Callie was completely different. Despite having shared a few passionate kisses, she seemed hesitant and cautious, which made him act in kind. Yet today she'd surprised the hell out of him when she'd agreed to jump off the cliff and then invited him over for dinner.

He'd laughed when she'd peppered him with questions on the way up the trail.

"Will it hurt when we hit the water? What if I don't come back up?"

"Callie," he'd said. "Don't worry. You're going to love it. Trust me."

And she had, although she'd clutched his hand so tightly that he still had red marks from her nails digging into his skin. He hadn't minded at all. When they'd sprung up out of the water, she'd been so excited she'd jumped into his arms and hugged him, yelling, "I did it! I did it!" until everyone in the vicinity started laughing and cheering.

He'd decided it was one of those moments that he'd never forget as long as he lived.

Now, as he prepared to knock on her door, he wondered if they were about to share another moment like that. He gave himself a silent pep talk (or more accurately, a talking down) like he'd been doing for the past hour or so.

It's just dinner. She's in charge. Go with the flow and just enjoy her company.

Glancing down at his watch, he saw it was five fifty-five. He hadn't wanted to come over too early or be late, so this was the perfect timing. He lifted his right hand and knocked.

"Coming," she called out.

Maybe later? Stop that!

She opened the door, and he froze. He'd seen her in dresses before, but this one was amazing. She usually covered her cleavage, but tonight it was on display due to the deep V-neck of the dress. There was just enough skin showing to make her look sexy and classy at the same time. The dress hugged her waist, which made him want to do the same, and the hem stopped at mid-thigh, showing the perfect amount of leg. He glanced down at her shoes and realized why she appeared taller than usual. Her strappy sandals were probably three inches high, and her bright pink toes peeked out at him.

"Chase? Would you like to come in?"

Hell yeah! "Yes. Thanks."

She giggled. "What are you thanking me for?"

His brain was scrambled, and who knew what might come out? "For the invitation. Dinner smells great."

"I hope you like stir-fry," she said, turning and walking to the kitchen.

He followed a few steps behind, admiring her backside and tan legs.

"I do. I brought the wine." He set it down on the kitchen counter, feeling like he'd just relinquished his security blanket. He hadn't realized how tightly he'd been holding it until then.

"Can you get down the wine glasses? They're too high for me to reach."

"Of course."

He took out two glasses while she put the finishing touches on their meal.

"You really didn't have to go to all this trouble. We could have gone out to eat." He'd said it even though he'd been thrilled she'd asked him there.

"It wasn't any trouble. This is a simple dish to make, and I was in the mood for a homecooked meal anyway."

What else are you in the mood for? "Can I set the table?"

"Sure."

He was glad to have something to do with his hands; otherwise, who knew where they might roam?

As they worked around each other in the kitchen, he was constantly aware of her presence and the scent of her perfume. He was glad he'd worn cologne after all now that he smelled it on her too.

There were no candles, soft music, or dim lighting, but the scene felt intimate anyway. It was just the two of them having dinner together, thousands of miles away from home and their everyday lives. It was peaceful and intoxicating at the same time.

"How about a toast?" he said once they were seated and he'd poured the wine.

"To my jumping?"

He shook his head. "Not just that. To Kauai and to us meeting here. I'm glad I met you, Callie."

She smiled sweetly, and they clinked glasses before raising them to their lips. *Lips. Callie's lips. Oh God. He was in deep trouble.*

He'd set the plates in such a way that he wouldn't be staring directly at her all through dinner. He hadn't been sure he could handle it. She was sitting to his left, at the head of the table, and he was facing the window with a view of the ocean.

"This is delicious," he said after a few minutes.

"I'm glad you like it. I have my grandmother to thank for teaching me how to cook."

"You must really miss her."

"I do. But oddly enough, I'm starting to feel better. She knew exactly what she was doing by making me come here."

"I'm glad it's helping."

"You deserve some of the credit too," she said.

He jerked his head up. "Me?"

She nodded. "You've helped me come of out of my shell. I know for a fact that I never would have jumped off that cliff if it weren't for you."

"Good thing it turned out okay, then. I wouldn't have wanted to take credit if you were lying in traction at the hospital instead."

"If that had happened, we wouldn't be having dinner together."

"I'd be spoon-feeding you Jell-O instead."

They laughed, and he felt himself loosening up. Never mind that he was on his second glass of wine.

"More?" he asked, holding up the bottle.

"Sure."

He poured and then set down the bottle. Their plates were empty, and he wondered, *Now what?*

"Would you like another helping?"

"No thanks."

"How about dessert? I have chocolate cake."

"Maybe later."

"Okay."

"I'll help you clean up."

"You don't have to."

"My mom and sister would be disappointed in me if I didn't. So yes, I have to."

She laughed, and they both stood up to clear the plates.

They worked side by side in the kitchen, but something about it felt different this time. There was a charge in the air, and they both knew it but weren't acknowledging it.

"We could take our wine into the living room," she suggested after they'd finished cleaning.

He nodded because suddenly he was tongue-tied. He topped off both their glasses, and then they went and sat down on the couch. He left a respectable distance between them and took another fortifying drink of wine while she got comfortable. When she crossed her legs and her dress rode up a little, he quickly looked away, but it didn't stop him from saying, "You look really pretty tonight. I like your dress."

"Thank you," she said, brightening. "Quinn gets the credit since she picked it out."

He shook his head. "But you're the one wearing it."

She smiled and swallowed hard. "I like your outfit too."

"This old thing?"

She giggled. "You're not wearing your glasses."

"My *sexy* glasses, you mean?"

She nodded. "You still look sexy without them."

Whoa. Didn't see that coming. "Thanks."

He watched her take a deep sip of wine before setting the glass on a coaster. "I'm really bad at this," she said, looking at him apologetically.

He set his glass down and moved a little closer. "Bad at what?"

"Seducing a man. Seducing you."

Am I hearing right? Did I get too much water in my ears in the shower? "You're seducing me?"

"Trying to," she said, looking down at her hands.

It was too much. He couldn't hold back anymore. "Look at me, Callie."

She tipped her head up and met his eyes. He hoped like hell she could see his desire there, because he was overflowing with it.

"Consider me seduced."

Chapter 27

Her eyes went wide, and when he held out his arms, she practically flew into them. In fact, she crashed into him so hard that he fell backward on the couch, taking her down with him.

"Sorry," she said. "I told you I wasn't good at this."

"Stop talking and kiss me," he growled.

So, she did because that was all she'd been able to think about all day. She tipped her head down and tasted his luscious lips, where the wine still lingered.

His arms went around her waist, locking her in and aligning their hips. When she slipped her tongue in his mouth, he groaned, and she felt him harden beneath her.

Maybe I'm not so bad at this after all, she thought as she wriggled against him.

His hands skimmed up her back and then cupped her head, and he started massaging her scalp. It felt like when she got her hair washed at the salon, only a million times better.

"Mmmm," she mumbled against his lips.

He chuckled. "You like that?"

"Um-hmm."

"Tell me what else you like."

Her eyes popped open. "Can I write it down instead?"

He burst out laughing. "What?"

"I'm so much better at writing than speaking."

Removing his hands from her hair, he ran them down her arms, leaving a trail of goosebumps in their wake. "Close your eyes and pretend you're writing."

"This is silly."

"I want to know what makes you feel good, Callie."

"You. You make me feel good."

That must have been a good answer, because he moved his hands around to her back and started kissing her again. This time, he pressed soft closed-mouth kisses to the corners of her lips, her chin, and even the tip of her nose. She loved every second of it.

Her body had begun responding to him long before the first kiss, and now she felt damp between her legs. As if he could sense her heightened state, he placed his fingers on the top of her zipper and glanced up at her for permission.

"Yes," she whispered. One-word sentences, she was capable of—for the moment.

He stopped kissing her and slowly peeled the zipper down, keeping his eyes on hers the entire time. As her back was exposed, the cool air brushed over her bare skin and made her squirm. She smiled down at him, wondering what his reaction would be when he discovered she wasn't wearing a bra.

"Do you want to stay here?" he asked, his voice sounding strained, almost like he was in pain.

With how hard his erection was, she could understand why. Or maybe not, since she wasn't a man and had no idea how it really felt.

"Do you?"

"Here we go again."

She laughed.

"Here is fine." When she started to sit up, he looked confused, but she motioned for him to stay put.

Balancing herself on his hips, she hooked her fingers into the straps of her dress and started pulling them down.

Chase sucked in a ragged breath as she revealed her bare breasts to him. "You didn't wear a bra," he stated as if he couldn't believe his good fortune.

She shook her head, warming under his intense gaze. Her nipples protruded sharply, begging for his touch, and luckily, she didn't have long to wait.

"Pretty," he said, cupping her breasts in his hands.

It had been a long time since she'd experienced this, and her desire was so intense she thought she would burst. He plucked her nipples, and she tipped her head back and moaned, louder than she'd intended to.

"I found something else you like," he said with a sexy grin.

He kept at it, alternating between massaging her breasts with his palms and teasing her nipples. Looking down she realized she was moving against his hips, effectively riding him like a bull.

"You're so sexy, Callie."

She shook her head, but it wasn't so much in response to his compliment as it was trying to keep herself in check. If they kept this up, it wouldn't be long at all, and...

Suddenly he sat up too, bringing them chest to chest and eye to eye. "Let's go to the bedroom."

She nodded, and he lifted her into his arms and carried her down the hall.

When he set her feet on the floor of her bedroom, she froze for a second.

"Everything okay?"

"Yes."

"Good. Let me finish undressing you."

Chasing Forever

She almost argued, thinking it only fair that he remove his clothes too. But his hands were already on her, and she felt too good to make him stop.

Her dress was open to the waist, and he carefully tugged it over her hips and down her legs. She stepped out of it, and he laid it at the end of the bed before coming to stand in front of her again.

She expected him to make quick work of removing her panties and sandals, but instead, he drew her up against him and kissed her deeply.

The kiss was wonderful, as all his kisses were, but she wanted more. She wanted to see and feel *all* of him. Taking a step back, she pulled up on his shirt, which was neatly tucked into his shorts. "I want this off."

"The lady speaks!"

She shot him a look that was half scowl, half smile, and he quickly pulled his shirt over his head and tossed it aside. "Better?"

"Um-hmm. But I've already seen your chest," she said, rubbing her hands over his pecs.

"You'd like to see more?"

"Would I be standing here in my underwear if I didn't?"

"There's my sassy girl."

He grinned and placed his hands on the button of his shorts. While he was unzipping them, she started to take off her sandals, but he placed a hand on her arm to stop her.

"Leave those on."

"But they might poke you."

"Don't care."

The sound of his shorts hitting the floor was like an explosion, and she looked down at his gray boxer briefs. She wished she could thank whoever had invented this style of men's underwear. They hugged his body like a second skin and showcased every hard, male inch of him.

"Good choice?" he said with a gruff laugh.

"Excellent choice."

She was expecting them to move on to the final reveal, but apparently, he had other plans. He hauled her into his arms, and she wrapped her legs around his waist while he backed them up to the bed.

He lifted her with such ease that she almost made a short joke, but she decided not to. He gently laid her down and then climbed over her on all fours, trapping her in the best possible way.

He started to say something, but she reached up and placed a finger over his lips. "You don't need to ask. I'm good, we're good, everything's good."

"Well, good."

They both laughed, but when he slipped his fingers into the sides of her panties, the smile froze on her face. *This is it. I'm really doing this. Go me!*

Still kneeling, Chase slid her panties down her legs and over her sandals, being careful not to snag them. Then he ran his hands up her inner thighs and gently nudged them apart.

She squirmed when he paused and looked at her most intimate spot, but more from need than nerves.

"Chase…"

"Yeah?"

"I need…"

"Tell me. I'll do whatever you want."

"Your hand, your mouth, or your…"

He didn't make her finish the sentence, and his mouth was right there, covering her and infusing her with warmth. He licked, flicked, and kissed her senseless until she was bucking beneath him.

It was so good that a few more licks would take her over the edge, but she wasn't ready to go there yet, not without him.

She'd threaded her hands in his hair, and now she gave it a tug.

He glanced up at her with concern. "Stop?"

"Get naked," she demanded. Then, deciding she'd sounded a bit dominatrixy, she added, "Please."

He chuckled and quickly moved off the bed. Finding his shorts, he pulled a condom out of the back pocket and tossed it on the bed. She considered opening it to save time, but then he started peeling off his boxer/briefs, and she had to watch.

Coming up on her elbows, she licked her lips when he revealed the magnificence he'd been concealing.

In romance novels, the heroine often exclaimed about how big the hero was, but in this case, it wasn't fiction! "Wow."

He came back over her with a huge smile on his face to match his other *big* part. "Found something else you like?"

"Uh, yeah!"

He sat back on his haunches and pointed to the condom. "Do you want to do the honors, or should I?"

"You can. I'll just sit here and stare if that's okay?"

"It's awesome. I like you looking at me like that."

"Like what?"

"Like you can't wait for me to be inside you."

She sucked in a breath because it was true.

She watched him roll the condom down his length, and then he crawled back over her, leaned down, and kissed her lips. She loved kissing him, but she still wanted more. Wrapping her arms around his waist, she tried pulling him down, but he barely budged.

Tearing her lips away, she scowled. "You're purposely teasing me."

"Am I?"

"I'm not playing this game with you."

He smirked and trailed a hand down the side of her body, which made her shiver again. "I'm just making sure you're ready for me."

"I'm ready already!"

"Let me check." With that, he skimmed his hand over her abdomen and lower until he touched her damp folds.

"See? I'm ready," she said, though her voice had lost its edge.

"Still checking," he said and then dipped a finger inside.

She arched up, chasing it as he swirled it around and flicked it over her most sensitive spot.

At present, Chase seemed like the perfect name for him. He was driving her insane with this cat-and-mouse game.

But she'd lost the will to fight as he explored her with his hand and gazed down at her with his gorgeous green eyes. She was literally putty in his hands, which might have scared her if she weren't so turned on she couldn't see straight.

"Chase..."

"I think you're ready now."

He lined himself up at her entrance and slowly guided himself inside, one amazing inch at a time.

Then he began to move. He held onto her hip for leverage and thrust forward, and she hooked a leg over his back, opening herself up even more. She was vaguely aware that the heel of her sandal was digging into his butt, yet he didn't seem to mind.

"Callie," he said on a puff of air. "I'm not gonna last."

"Me either," she said, panting.

Voicing their mutual need seemed to crack them both wide open, and they moaned and groaned while they ground out their release.

He continued to pulsate inside her as they came down, and she carefully extracted her heel from his butt.

"Ahhh," he said against her neck.

"I know. That had to hurt."

He popped his head up and looked at her questioningly.

"My heel in your ass."

He chuckled and shook his head. "I meant ahhh, as in that was awesome. I barely even noticed your heel in my butt. But now that you mention it..." He reached around and massaged his butt cheek, and then he slowly withdrew and rolled off to the side.

She turned her head toward him and smiled. "I agree. It was pretty awesome."

"I'll go take care of this," he said, motioning to the condom. "Be right back."

She watched him pad naked to the bathroom and close the door behind him.

She shimmied against the damp sheets and stared up at the ceiling, replaying what had just happened. She waited for the doubts or worries to creep in, but amazingly, they didn't. Maybe it would happen later when she was alone. But right then, her body was too flooded with endorphins for any negative feelings to take hold. In fact, all she could think about was how wonderful she felt.

It was a euphoric feeling, similar to when she'd jumped off the cliff earlier. She hadn't considered jumping again, but she'd like to have Chase again. In fact, her body was already responding just thinking about it.

Waiting for him to come back out, she wondered if he felt the same...

Chapter 28

Chase eyed himself in the bathroom mirror and mouthed, "Wow!" He'd forgotten what good sex felt like, and now that he'd been reminded, he never wanted it to end. Problem was, it had to. Not now and not for the next few weeks, but soon enough. Neither of them had any intention of starting something and certainly not of continuing it once they'd returned to their real lives in Michigan.

Real life, Michigan, divorce attorney—three things he'd run away from. He'd never imagined he'd be running to something, or more specifically, someone. But now that he'd found her, how could he let her go?

He'd discovered the answer to one of his burning questions: would Callie be as passionate and uninhibited in bed as the romance heroines she wrote about? The answer was a resounding yes! He was getting aroused just thinking about it, and he already wanted her again. He finished drying his hands and then ran them through his rumpled hair, recalling her tugging on it at during their lovemaking. He stood there for another minute, willing his erection to go down, when suddenly Callie called out.

"Everything okay in there?"

Shit. How long had he been standing there in a maelstrom of shock, elation, and arousal?

"Coming," he said and then winced at the connotation.

When he opened the bathroom door and saw her, he concluded he hadn't been the only one thinking about round two. She was sitting up against the headboard, still naked down to her toes—she'd even taken her sandals off. *Interesting.*

Then she crooked her finger, inviting him to come and join her. *Really? Is this my lucky day or what?*

He waltzed across the room with confidence, his erection leading the way, and crawled onto the bed. "Again?" he asked, just to be sure.

"If you're up for it, which it looks like you are." She glanced down and then gave him a seductive smile.

He lay on his side, propped up on an elbow, and reached out to finger her pretty, dark hair. "You're blowing my mind right now."

"How so?" She trailed a fingertip up and down his bare arm. Crazy how the slightest touch from her turned him on.

"You constantly surprise me. First, jumping off the cliff, and now…"

"Yes?" She'd moved her hand to his chest and was drawing tight circles around his nipples. Who knew a man's nipples could be so sensitive?

"You're just a lot different in private."

"Weren't you the one who said we all show a certain persona to the world that may or may not be the whole story?"

"I think you added the story part."

"That's the writer in me. Sorry."

"Don't be. You're an excellent writer." *Uh-oh.*

She'd been trailing her finger down his chest, toward his goods, and then she paused. Narrowing her eyes and cocking her head, she said, "How do you know that?"

"I…um…I don't know for sure. I'm just assuming so."

She obviously wasn't buying it. Moving away from him, she sat up against the headboard again, but this time, she covered herself with one of the throw pillows.

Chase sat up too, but he didn't bother with modesty. Her eyes were locked on his, and he'd already started deflating.

"Callie…"

"How do you know what kind of writer I am, Chase? Has someone you know read my books? Your sister, maybe?"

Damnit! He never should have kept this from her, but it was too late now. He slowly nodded.

"So, you know? You know everything about me, but you never told me? Why?" Her voice was rising with every word, and a vein bulged at the side of her neck. He thought that only happened with men.

He held up a hand. "Hold on. First of all, I don't know *everything* about you, but I want to."

"Why didn't you just come out and ask?"

"I have, but every time I brought up your writing, you shut me down. It's almost like you're embarrassed or ashamed, and I don't understand why. Most people I know who've written books like to shout it from the rafters."

"I'm not most people," she hissed.

"I'm learning that."

"What else have you *learned*?"

He thought about getting up to get some clothes on but was afraid she'd tell him to keep walking and never come back. It was hard to believe that just a few minutes ago, they'd been wrapped in each other's arms and he'd been buried deep inside her. Her current posture said she could hardly stand the sight of him. He had to fix this.

Taking a deep breath, he said, "I did a search. There are a lot of other authors named Callie Cooper, by the way."

She scowled.

"Anyway, I finally found you by your author photo. It's a great picture of you."

"Don't do that, Chase. Don't treat me like one of your little bikini-clad girlfriends from the pool. You can't charm me that easily."

He stared at her for a moment and shook his head, anger and disappointment rising up in him. Why was this all his fault? All he'd wanted to do was get to know her better, and now this. He pushed himself off the bed, walked around to where his clothes were, and started shoving them on.

"I still don't get it. From everything I read, you're a successful romance author with an avid fan base, including my sister, who's read every book you've ever written. Why can't you just own that?"

"This isn't about my profession. It's about you sneaking around behind my back and lying. When were you going to tell me, or weren't you? You probably thought it didn't matter because we'll never see each other again after Hawaii. Am I right?"

He looked down at the carpet and shook his head. "I don't know. I wanted to tell you a few times, but I didn't. I figured you had your reasons for not telling me you were a romance author, so I decided to let it go. But if you're ashamed of what you do, you shouldn't be."

"I'm proud of what I do," she said, slapping her hand against the mattress. "I'm a damn good writer."

"I know. I read two of your books." He'd blurted it out without thinking, but he was glad he had. Even if she hated him and never wanted to see him again, at least he didn't have any more secrets. Or did he? *You haven't been forthright about your own profession.* But now was not the time.

She stilled, and her eyes went wide.

"That's right, and I'm not sorry. I thought reading one of your books might help me get to know you better. That was my only motivation, to know you better. So, there you have it. Full disclosure. Guilty as charged."

"You actually read my books? Which ones? When?"

She looked a little less angry, but he was still wary.

"I asked my sister for a recommendation, and she told me to start at the beginning of the series, so I did."

"And then you *kept* reading?"

"I'm a wuss. Sue me." Lawyer-speak often weaseled its way into his conversations even when he didn't want it to.

"Chase..."

He started backing up to the bedroom door. "No. You know what. I was wrong, okay? Wrong to go behind your back and wrong about a lot of other things. I'm leaving now."

She started to move like she might try to stop him, but he turned and stalked out, knowing there was nothing left to say.

He heard her call his name, but he was out the door before she emerged from the bedroom. Since his wallet and keys were in his pockets, he decided to take off for a while and clear his head. Besides, he wasn't ready for another confrontation. He needed distance, and for the first time, he wished they weren't living next door to each other.

He got into his rental car with no destination in mind. It was already getting late, but he knew he wouldn't be able to sleep anyway. He'd just drive until he got tired and then turn around and go back.

He backed out of the parking space and sped off, forcing himself not to look in the rearview mirror. He didn't want to know if she'd come outside after him or, worse, if she hadn't. It didn't matter either way. The damage was done. She probably thought the worst of him now—that he was a lying, scheming, conniving SOB who didn't care about anything other than getting in her pants (or up her dress, as it were).

Chasing Forever

If only she'd known the true story—that he'd genuinely liked, admired, and been attracted to her long before they'd made love. That, to him, she was more beautiful and sexier than any of the "bikini-clad girlfriends" that he'd met at the pool. And if he had the chance, he'd do everything over the right way so that instead of arguing, they might still be wrapped in each other's arms, loving each other all night long.

Chapter 29

Callie had hastily thrown on a robe and run to her front door, but it was too late. Chase had peeled off into the night, and she stood there until his taillights disappeared. Sighing, she went back inside and flopped onto the couch, noticing they'd left their wine glasses on the coffee table. She picked up her glass and took a sip, but it was lukewarm, and she preferred it chilled. She thought about getting up for a fresh glass but realized it was futile. No amount of wine would make her forget what had happened.

She'd screwed up big time. Her initial shock and anger had worn off, and now she was left feeling cold, lonely, and ashamed. Chase wasn't the only one who'd dug up information and kept it a secret.

She needed to come clean too, but she hadn't gotten the chance. After explaining himself, Chase had raced out of there so fast she'd had no hope of catching him. Maybe it was for the best.

Confessing her own secrets might have made a bad situation worse. Anyway, what did it really matter? In the end, they'd be going their separate ways. This was just a vacation fling, a temporary escape, and in her case, an experiment of sorts. Too bad the experiment would be short-lived. Chase probably wouldn't want anything to do with her now that she'd gone off on him like that, and she wouldn't blame him.

He'd been right about one thing. She'd been cagey about her profession but not for the reasons he'd thought. She wasn't ashamed or embarrassed about being a romance author. She was proud of it. But she hadn't wanted him to discover she was using him as her muse. The less she talked about writing the better, or so she'd thought.

She wondered if her story would stall out again. She'd stopped writing in the middle of a sex scene, and then they'd actually had sex. That in itself would be a major source of inspiration, but now she'd sabotaged herself.

Sitting there in the dark, staring at their empty wine glasses and recalling every detail of their lovemaking, she felt incredibly sad. Being with Chase had brought her complete and utter happiness, something she hadn't felt in a long time, and then she'd gone and ruined it.

If only he hadn't driven away. Then she'd have gone next door and apologized. But it was late, and who knew when he'd come back? Finally, she got up and took the glasses to the kitchen. A few minutes later, she crawled back into bed, the sheets still warm and smelling like him. She closed her eyes and inhaled deeply, knowing she was in for a restless night.

Two days later, Chase still hadn't returned to his condo, and now she'd become concerned. What if he'd been so blinded by fury that he'd gotten into a car accident? He could be lying in a hospital bed somewhere, and she'd have no idea. They'd never exchanged phone numbers, and she doubted he'd have asked the hospital personnel to contact her anyway.

There was also the possibility that he'd left for home, but wouldn't he have come back for his belongings first? None of it made sense, but she was determined to find him. First, she called the local hospitals, which turned out to be a dead end—thank God. Next, she went to the resort office and asked if he'd checked out.

Initially, the woman at the desk was reluctant to give out any information, but when Callie said she feared for his safety, the woman folded. She clicked a few keys on her computer and then said, "He hasn't checked out yet."

Afterward, Callie wasn't sure what to do other than contact his law office, but she nixed that idea. She'd hate to unnecessarily get his family into a panic over his whereabouts. Maybe he'd decided to explore one of the other islands. It would be a quick hop by plane to any of them, but wouldn't he have wanted to pack a bag first?

She hadn't known him that long, but he didn't seem like the type to want to wear the same clothes for three days. She considered calling Hawaiian Airlines to ask if he'd booked a flight, but even if he had, then what? She didn't plan on chasing after him, and how would she find him anyway?

After lamenting to Quinn, she realized there was nothing more she could do. Quinn's theory was that he'd slunk away with his tail between his legs and soon he'd return to grovel at her feet.

But Callie didn't need him to grovel. She just wanted to know he was safe, and after that, she'd leave him alone if that was what he wanted.

As she suspected, her writing came to a screeching halt. She sat in front of the laptop each day and tried to write something, anything, but nothing felt right. She'd type a few sentences and delete them, type and delete, until finally, she'd walked away in frustration.

She was angry but mostly at herself for letting Chase's disappearance affect her so much. If he didn't want to be found, he wouldn't be, and she needed to accept that.

Finally, on the third day, she decided to stop wallowing and do something to distract herself. She hadn't wanted to stray too far from the resort in case Chase reappeared, so she settled for going to the pool.

She put on her black one-piece because who was she trying to impress? Then she packed her beach bag with the usual supplies, slipped on her flip-flops, and headed out.

It was another glorious day, with brilliant blue skies, a slight breeze, and comfortable temperatures. As she walked to the pool, she realized she'd been taking the pleasant weather for granted. All too soon, she'd be back in Michigan, and even though it would technically be spring, they could still be hit with a snowstorm.

Determined to enjoy the day, she went into the pool area and selected a lounge chair that offered some shade. So far, she hadn't gotten sunburned, but she didn't want to risk it. After she set down her bag and settled into the chair with sunglasses on and book in hand, she glanced around the pool deck.

There was the usual variety of people: families with children, some elderly folks, and a few singles. In the opposite corner from her, she spotted Sara and the muscly guy who had replaced Chase that day on the beach. Sara was sitting between his legs on the lounge chair, and her *friend* was massaging sunscreen onto her back.

Callie watched them for a few more minutes, sure that Sara wouldn't even recognize her without Chase. Besides, she was too focused on the guy she was with, which was as it should be. Seeing them together made Callie a tad envious. What she wouldn't give for Chase to be rubbing lotion on her right then, or rubbing something else…

Then, as if imagining it had conjured him up, she spotted him opening the pool gate, cool as you please, like nothing in the world was wrong.

She almost bolted out of her chair, but then she talked herself out of it. She didn't want to cause a scene at the pool with all these witnesses. Besides, he might not even want to talk to her.

Then he stepped through the gate and held it open for someone else to come in behind him.

Callie stiffened. It was a woman, of course. A young, attractive woman with medium brown hair, a curvy build, and a pretty smile. She was looking up at Chase and beaming, and jealousy struck again.

Who was this woman, and where had she come from? Callie hadn't seen her around the resort before, not that she'd seen all the guests, but she was pretty observant. This woman was someone who would have stood out.

Her brain was awhirl with emotions, and she wasn't sure which one it would land on. She sank further down in the chair and held up her book to block her face. She was glad she'd put her hair in a ponytail and was wearing a ball cap. It had been a last-minute decision, but now it might help disguise her. She hugged her knees to her chest so he wouldn't recognize her bathing suit and shoved her beach bag under the chair. It was the best she could do on short notice.

It was mid-afternoon, and the pool deck was getting crowded. There were a few empty chairs near her and two next to Sara, but she doubted he'd choose to sit there.

Then she heard Sara's voice. "Hi, Chase! Come over and meet my boyfriend, Josh."

Callie lowered her book some and saw Chase reluctantly walk over to them with his new lady in tow. He shook hands with Josh and then introduced them to his *whoever*, but unlike Sara, he hadn't spoken loud enough for Callie to hear.

It was obvious Sara had forgiven Chase for ditching her that day. *Too bad I don't forgive that easily*, Callie thought.

Sara motioned to the empty chairs beside her, but Chase shook his head and turned and pointed across the pool.

Did he see me? I hope not! Callie held up her book again for added insurance.

Funny how her body was so in tune with his already. She felt his presence as he and his guest came closer, and then she heard them plunk down in the empty chairs in her row.

They were separated by a couple with two young children who were playing and talking loudly. Callie prayed the kids would provide enough of a distraction to keep Chase from noticing her. Good thing she'd gone to the bathroom before coming to the pool. She didn't plan on getting up from the chair unless she absolutely had to.

A few minutes later, when things had quieted down some, she ventured a peek over the top of her book. Chase was standing in the shallow end of the pool, but he was looking at his *whoever* and trying to convince her to get in the pool.

"It's not cold," he said. "Come on in."

"I will in a few. I want to read for a while."

"You can read later."

"Just a chapter or two. I promise."

He muttered something and then dove underneath the water and swam across to the deep end of the pool.

Callie was intrigued, and for a moment, she forgot her plight. Whenever somebody talked about reading, she got a thrill. It was like belonging to a club, and she was an avid member. She couldn't help lowering her novel a bit more to see what Chase's *whoever* was reading.

She glanced over, and her mouth fell open. She'd recognize that book cover anywhere—it was one of hers! In her excitement, she accidentally fumbled her own book, and it fell to the ground with a thud. The noise probably wouldn't have alerted the woman, but when Callie leaned over to pick up the book, the chair went with her. The next thing she knew, she was sprawled on the ground next to her damaged novel, and the chair was tipped on its side.

"Ohmigod! Are you okay? Here, let me help you up," Chase's *whoever* said, offering her hand.

Keeping her head down, Callie replied, "No thanks. I'm fine."

"But you're bleeding."

Sure enough, she'd skinned both knees, and they were bleeding like she was a little kid who'd fallen off her bike.

"Callie?" Chase rushed up to them, dripping wet.

Oh no. It can't possibly get worse than this!

"Callie? Callie Cooper? The author?" The woman gaped at her, seemingly having forgotten about her bleeding knees.

"Let me help you," Chase demanded and practically pushed the other woman aside.

"I've got it," Callie hissed.

But Chase ignored her. Placing his arms under hers, he carefully lifted her to her feet.

"Don't just stand there. Fix her chair!" he barked at the woman.

Nice way to talk to your new girlfriend, Callie thought and scowled at him.

The woman had finally gathered her wits and ran around to right the chair. She stood by while Chase carefully lowered Callie into it and then leaned over to assess the damage.

But it was more than her knees that hurt. How could he bring another woman around so soon? And why here, where he knew Callie might be? Was he really that insensitive? Had she misread him?

"Miranda, run inside and check my suitcase. I think I have some bandages in there. Bring a damp cloth too."

Miranda? Why did that name sound familiar?

"Be right back," she said and hurried off.

Callie opened her mouth to speak, but Chase beat her to it.

"My sister. Your number one fan."

Her shoulders slumped with relief, but all was not forgiven.

"What happened?" he asked, rubbing his hands up and down her lower legs, carefully avoiding her knees.

She tried not to think about how wonderful it felt to have his hands on her again.

"I glanced over and saw your sister reading one of my novels, and I...I don't know exactly. I got excited, and then I dropped my book. When I leaned over to pick it up, I fell. It was a stupid mistake."

He looked directly into her eyes and softly smiled. "I'm sorry it happened."

"Me too."

She had a feeling they were referring to more than her fall. She was just about to ask where he'd been when Miranda came racing toward them with a box of bandages and a washcloth.

She handed them to Chase, who immediately went to work patching Callie up.

"Quite a memorable way to meet one of your favorite authors, huh?" he said over his shoulder.

"I'm Miranda, Chase's one and only sister and your number one fan," Miranda stated.

Callie smiled and offered her hand, which Miranda eagerly shook. "I don't usually meet my fans this way. Sorry."

"Don't apologize. I'm just so happy to finally meet you, and I'm glad you weren't seriously hurt."

"Just my pride," Callie said.

"There. Good as new," Chase proclaimed, sitting back on his haunches.

"Thanks. I didn't mean to cause so much trouble, especially with your sister visiting." She wondered if he'd picked up on the double meaning and hoped he had.

"She just arrived this morning, but I planned on introducing you."

"I didn't give him much notice, but he offered to meet me in Oahu and fly over here with me, so I took him up on it."

"Oahu?" Callie said, directing her question to Chase.

"It's a long story..."

"I'd like to hear it," she said.

"Maybe over dinner?" Miranda inserted.

"Give her a break. She's hurt," Chase scolded.

"I'll be fine, and I'd like to get to know your 'one and only sister,'" Callie said.

Miranda looked thrilled, and Chase less so, but he glanced between the two women and caved.

"Fine. But I'm driving."

Miranda rolled her eyes at him. "Men!"

Chapter 30

Chase wasn't sure going out to dinner with his sister and Callie was such a great idea. He couldn't get a word in edgewise, and it was driving him crazy. He had so much to say to Callie, yet Miranda wouldn't stop gushing, and Callie seemed equally smitten with her. It was maddening!

"So, how do you come up with ideas for your novels?" Miranda asked in between bites of salmon.

"I'm sure Callie doesn't want to talk about this all night long, sis."

"It's okay. I like talking about books anytime," Callie said.

Chase sighed and took another swig of beer. He might as well settle into it.

"I find inspiration everywhere," Callie began. "From a trip to the grocery store to a trip to Hawaii." She shot Chase a glance that sent a spark of desire straight to his... *Not now! My sister's here.*

"Wow. That's so cool," Miranda said. "And your characters seem so real. It's like, if I met them in real life, I'd want to hang out with them."

Callie smiled and then took a long drink of her fruity cocktail.

Is she nervous or just being humble? Chase couldn't imagine why she'd be nervous talking to her "number one fan" about her books, but there was something in her expression...

"I'm often asked if my characters are based on real people, and for the most part, they're not. However, it's almost impossible not to draw from some of the experiences I've had and some of the people I've...had contact with."

Now we're getting somewhere.

"Oh really? Like who?" He was extremely curious about her answer.

"All kinds of people," she said, flapping her hand dismissively.

"So, you weave real experiences and people into your stories," Miranda said, clearly enthralled by the conversation.

Callie nodded. "Add in a healthy dose of imagination, and I've got myself a book."

"Hmmm," Chase said, eyeing her closely.

She gave him a brief smile and averted her eyes.

She was still hiding something, and he was determined to find out what it was. But first, he had some groveling to do. He shouldn't have run out on her that night and stayed away as long as he had. It was a bonehead move, and he wanted to apologize. But with Miranda there, he wasn't sure when he'd get the chance.

After he'd left that night, he'd listened to a voice mail from Miranda telling him she was coming to visit. She'd be there in two days, and she'd rattled off her flight information. He should have known he couldn't hold her off for long, especially after she'd found out about Callie. If only the timing had been better.

He'd decided to stay overnight at a hotel near the airport on Kauai. The next day, he hopped a plane to Oahu, where he waited to greet his sister. He hadn't bothered returning to the resort to pack a bag. Instead, he went shopping in Honolulu for a change of clothes and some toiletries.

He spent the day roaming around the city and thinking about everything that had transpired with Callie. He realized what a fool he'd been on so many levels. But most of all, he wished they'd exchanged phone numbers so he could call her. She might not have answered, but still, he'd wanted to reach out to her.

Finally, after wandering around the city all day, he stayed at another hotel near the airport and greeted Miranda when she arrived the next day. She was surprised and happy to see him there until he explained that he and Callie had had a falling out.

He told her the bare minimum (leaving out their lovemaking) and then waited for her to weigh in, smack him, or both. To his surprise, she hugged him tight and said, "Aww. How sweet. You're in love."

"What?!" he replied, looking at her like she was crazy.

"Why else would you be so torn up about it? If she didn't matter to you, you wouldn't be here right now."

Chase cocked his head at her. "You just got here, and already the sun has fried your brain."

"Deflecting. Typical of you."

He sighed and followed her through the airport to claim her luggage. She was dressed to kill in high heels, a denim skirt, and a flowy blouse, looking fresh and pretty despite the long flight. He was glad she was there even if she was already being a pain in the ass.

Once they'd boarded the plane to Kauai, she'd started in on him. He'd been exhausted by the time they'd landed, but Miranda still looked fresh as a daisy as she chatted excitedly with Callie about books.

"I love all the men in your stories, but so far, my favorite is Simon," Miranda gushed.

"Why him?" Callie asked, looking genuinely curious.

"He's like the perfect blend of sweet and sexy. I just wanted to eat him up."

Chase paused with a fork halfway to his mouth. "I'm sitting right here."

Miranda and Callie laughed.

"I'm not a kid anymore," Miranda said. "It's not like I'm talking about sex or anything."

"Okay. You know what? Can we change the subject?" he said, scowling at his sister.

"I agree. How about telling me about you?" Callie said, smiling sweetly at Miranda.

For the next ten minutes, Chase listened to his sister rehash her life, telling stories that were mostly familiar to him. He zoned out a few times and gazed at Callie over his beer glass.

She looked much happier than when he'd left that night and at the pool. What he hadn't admitted yet was that he'd known she was there all along.

He'd spotted her immediately, but he could tell she hadn't wanted to be seen, so he'd pretended not to see her. It had been hard as hell to keep from going to her straight away and apologizing. But then Sara had called him over, and he'd had to endure being formally introduced to her new beau, which was the last thing he'd cared about.

Plus, he hadn't wanted Miranda to go bonkers when she met Callie for the first time. He'd wanted to ease her into it, but he should have realized there was no easing Miranda into anything. She was either all in or all out. She was born with only two speeds, but he loved her anyway.

"It's interesting that you and my brother have become friends," Miranda said, suddenly shifting gears.

Oh no. Where is she going with this?

"Miranda..."

"Why's that?" Callie asked, leaning forward with interest.

"Well, a divorce attorney and a romance writer—talk about opposites!" Miranda laughed and then rose from the table. "I have to visit the ladies' room. Be right back."

Nothing like dropping a bomb and then leaving. Chase watched her go and then slowly turned to face the music. But Callie didn't look the least bit surprised.

"I already knew," she said warily. "I looked you up on Google."

The irony of it struck a funny bone, and he busted out laughing. Once he started, he couldn't stop, and he realized he was causing a scene.

Callie glanced over at the people at the neighboring table and shrugged. But when she turned back to him, she was smiling. "You're not mad?"

"How could I be? I did the same thing to you."

"You told me you're an attorney, but you left out the divorce part. Why?"

"I don't know. I guess I didn't want you to think I was some asshole lawyer out to make a profit on other peoples' misery. And what my sister said about us being opposites—it's kind of true, isn't it?"

To his surprise, Callie shook her head. "I don't think we're so different. Not in the ways that count."

He didn't have time to absorb her comment because Miranda returned to the table, looking proud of herself and wearing fresh lipstick. He knew without a doubt she'd purposely stayed away long enough so they could talk, and he was grateful. There was still so much more he had to say, though.

They spent another hour at the restaurant, indulging in more drinks and dessert. The atmosphere had shifted again, and he felt better than he had in days. Between the food, the drinks, and the company, he felt satisfied and content.

Well, mostly, anyway. What he'd really like was to spend the rest of the evening with Callie alone. But that wasn't going to happen. He couldn't ditch his sister on her first night there, and she'd be staying with him for the next few days.

He was quiet on the drive back to the resort, while Miranda and Callie continued to talk books. When they got out of the car, he went around back to get Miranda's bags.

"It was really nice meeting you, Callie. I hope we'll get a chance to talk some more while I'm here," Miranda said. She gave Callie a hug and then turned to Chase and said, "Hand me the keys, and I'll let myself in."

"What about your bags?"

"You're the one with the muscles. You can bring them in."

He tossed her the keys and gave her an eye roll because he knew what she was doing. She was giving him another chance to be alone with Callie, and he'd take it.

"Your sister's so sweet," Callie said as he hefted her third bag from the car.

"Geez. Do all women pack this much for only a few days?"

She laughed. "You don't want to know how much I packed for this trip."

Yes, I do. I want to know everything about you. "Callie..."

"Your sister's waiting, Chase. We don't have time to talk now."

"I know, but there's one thing we can do."

"What is it?"

"Exchange phone numbers."

She laughed and then reached in her purse and pulled out her phone. "What's your number?"

He rattled it off and watched her enter it. "Send me a text when you get in so I'll have your number."

"Okay."

Somehow he managed to carry all his sister's bags to the front door while Callie walked by his side.

When they reached their porches, he paused. "I wish we could spend more time together tonight, but..."

"Miranda's here. I understand."

"Soon, though, okay?"

She nodded.

He glanced down at her mouth, wishing he could kiss it, but he was afraid it was too soon.

In a surprise move, Callie went up on her tiptoes and kissed his cheek. "I'm glad you're back," she said. "Now, go inside and be nice to your sister!"

Chapter 31

Callie didn't see much of Chase for the next few days, but she had plenty to do. Her muse was back, and she immediately went to work writing again. Oftentimes she'd work outside on the patio, where she could feel the breeze and enjoy the view. Overall, the writing conditions were ideal, and she'd made a lot of progress.

Since she and Chase had exchanged phone numbers, they'd been texting regularly. Most of the texts were simple, such as him asking how her writing was coming and her asking what he and Miranda were up to.

He'd been apologetic about his sister taking up so much of his time, but Callie understood. She missed him, though, and no amount of texting could make up for not seeing or talking to him in person.

One night, he called her instead of texting. It was late, and she'd been in bed reading.

"Hey. Is this too late to call?" he asked.

"Why are you whispering?"

"Because Miranda's right across the hall."

Callie giggled. "It's not too late. I was just lying here reading." *And thinking of you.*

"Me too."

"One of your crime novels?"

"No. One of yours."

"Oh." She shouldn't have been surprised since he'd admitted it, but it still caught her off guard.

"I have to admit, I'm a little...keyed up now."

She laughed. "One of those chapters, huh?"

"Mm-hmm. How do you do it? I don't mean do *it*. I mean write about *it*."

She shimmied under the blanket and sighed. "Lots of times, I close my eyes and picture the scene in my mind. I try and conjure up the emotions that the characters would be feeling and go from there."

"Well, you do a good job of it, because I'm feeling it right now!"

She was too, just from talking to him.

"I'm really sorry about what happened that night," she blurted out. She hadn't had the chance to apologize yet, and it had been eating her up inside. "I overreacted."

"We're both to blame. We were both keeping secrets," Chase replied. He went on to explain what had happened after he'd left. "I'm sorry too. It was wrong of me to leave like that."

"Let's put it behind us and make a fresh start."

"Great idea. Miranda's leaving soon."

"I know."

"She asked if you'd like to hang out with us tomorrow. Maybe drive up the coast, have lunch, hit a few souvenir shops?"

"Sounds fun."

"Good. Well, I should probably let you go..."

"One more thing."

"Yeah?"

"Can I have your email address?"

"My email?"

"Um-hmm. I wondered if you'd like to read a few chapters of my new book."

"I thought you said you don't let anyone read your first draft."

"I don't usually, but if you don't want to..."

"No. I mean yes. I'd like to read it."

"I still have a lot of editing to do before it's published."

"In other words, it's not perfect."

"Right."

"But it will be."

"I hope so."

"I know so."

After that, he gave her his email address, which she wrote down on the notepad beside her bed.

"Good thing you always have a notepad handy," he teased.

After they hung up, Callie realized she was smiling. She'd given it a lot of thought over the past few days and decided she wanted to share her writing with him. When she'd first started out, she'd taken great pains to hide it from him, but she was done hiding. She wanted him to know that he'd had a hand in the making of her story. Instead of just telling him, she wanted him to discover it for himself.

He was an intelligent man. It wouldn't take long to figure out that he was the inspiration behind her male hero, especially when it came to his physical description. He'd probably also recognize snippets of conversations they'd had, though she hadn't written them verbatim. The chapter she was most anxious for him to read, though, was the one where the characters made love for the first time.

If Chase felt all the feels from her other books, she imagined he'd feel them a hundred times over with that one. At least, she hoped so. Making love with him had been an eye-opening experience for her. It had happened after a long dry spell when she'd closed herself off to the possibilities of love and intimacy. Being with Chase had reminded her of all that was good in life and all that she still had to look forward to. Her future seemed brighter, but whether he would be a part of it remained to be seen.

She could easily envision dating him when they went back home, but she questioned if he felt the same. Maybe to him, this was just a vacation romance soon to be forgotten, but she'd never forget it. Aside from Chase, she had one other person to thank for the experience—Irene.

The next morning, she decided to change up her routine. Instead of lounging around in her pjs, sipping coffee, and writing, she decided to hike out to the cliff.

She got into her exercise clothes (which were worn more for comfort than exercise), donned her sneakers and sunglasses, and went out into the early morning air.

Partway down the path, she realized she hadn't brought her phone, but it didn't matter. There was only one person she needed to talk to right then, and that person was in heaven.

She passed a few people on the trail, mostly morning joggers like Chase. She wondered if she'd bump into him, but she hadn't heard any sounds from his unit that morning, so maybe he was sleeping in.

It was a lot easier to traverse the steep dirt trail with sneakers than flip-flops, and soon she was at the top, huffing a bit from the climb. *I should have been doing this every morning*, she thought. *Then I wouldn't be so winded.*

There weren't any cliff jumpers that early in the morning, and she picked her way along the rocky trail to where she and Chase had been before. The breeze was cool and ruffled her hair, but the sun was warm on her skin. She looked out over the expanse of ocean and exhaled. If only she could bottle this scene and take it back to Michigan.

In a way, though, she already had. She'd included her cliff-jumping experience in her new book and painted the picture of this exact view as she'd jumped. She smiled recalling how she'd clutched Chase's hand so tightly she'd left red marks and how he'd been so proud of her he hadn't minded.

She walked a little further until she found a boulder to sit on near the cliff's edge. It was far enough away from the trail to afford some privacy, which was what she wanted.

Hugging her legs to her chest and wrapping her arms around them, she glanced out to sea.

"Grandma? I hope you're listening, and maybe Grandpa is too. I just wanted to say thank you for giving me this precious gift. I can't express how much it's meant to me…"

She paused to swallow as her eyes welled up with tears. She hadn't known that would happen, and she hadn't brought tissues. So much for always being prepared.

"My muse is back, and that's mostly thanks to you. You knew that sending me here would help, and it did. But there's something else that's helped too. Or, I should say, someone."

She quickly glanced around, and not seeing anyone, she continued. "His name is Chase. Good name for a book hero, right? I gave him a different name in my book, but it's him, Grandma. He provided a lot of inspiration too."

A tear slipped down her cheek, and she swatted it away.

"I think you'd like him. He's tall and handsome and has the most gorgeous green eyes. But aside from that, he's sweet and caring, and...he's turned my world upside down in a good way."

The breeze picked up, and she wanted to believe it was Irene's way of responding. Hugging her legs a little tighter, she smiled through her tears.

"I'm not sure what the future holds, but he helped bring my smile back, and I wanted you to know. I love you, Grandma. Thank you so much for everything you've ever done for me. I still feel you even though you're not here."

She couldn't say any more because her throat had clogged up. She bent her head to her knees and let herself cry, but these tears were different from the ones she'd shed in the recent past. These were tears of sadness for her grandma not being there, gratitude for all that Irene had given her, and hope for a brighter future.

A few minutes later, she'd wiped her tears and was about to stand up when suddenly she felt a presence nearby. She jerked her head to the right and looked straight into a pair of brilliant green eyes. *Chase.*

Chapter 32

Chase hadn't realized it was her at first, but as he got closer, there was no mistaking her glossy dark hair and petite body perched on the rock. He almost called out to her, but the way she was sitting with her head down and hugging her knees, he didn't want to startle her. Was she meditating? Deep in thought about her book? Sad?

He couldn't tell until suddenly her head popped up, and she looked right at him. She'd been crying, and his heart dropped.

"Callie? Are you okay?" He moved closer, still unsure if his presence was welcomed.

She nodded and offered him a tentative smile. Then she scooted over on the rock and patted the space beside her.

It was an invitation he gladly took. He settled in, and because the surface of the rock was only so wide, their bodies touched from shoulder to knee. He slipped an arm around her waist and pulled her close.

"Didn't expect to see you here," he said. He'd gone out for his morning run a bit later than usual and had decided to run up the cliff trail to burn off some of the extra calories he'd consumed.

"I was compelled to come up here this morning," she said, her voice sounding a bit raw. "I wanted to talk to my grandmother."

"Oh, sweetheart," he said, the term of affection slipping out naturally. He wrapped his other arm around her front and squeezed.

"I'm okay. It was a good talk even though it was one-sided."

She gave a little laugh, which made him laugh too.

"What did you have to say, or is it too personal?"

She leaned her head against his chest, and he inhaled the sweet scent of her shampoo, suppressing the urge to nuzzle his nose in her hair.

"I thanked her for sending me here, or forcing me is more like it."

"I can think of worse things to be forced into."

"I miss her, Chase."

"I know. I bet she'd be so proud of you. You've been working hard on your new book, and hey, you jumped off this cliff. That had to earn you a few extra points!"

She glanced up at him with a smile. "You forgot one other thing."

He brushed her hair off her face. "What's that?"

"I met you."

He froze for a second, the loving look in her eyes stealing his breath.

"Sorry. Maybe you weren't ready to hear that."

"You just surprised me. Things haven't exactly been smooth between us."

"Do you mean perfect? Because nothing ever is, Chase. That's the beauty of it."

"Okay, you lost me."

She giggled and lifted a hand to his stubbly cheek. "Neither of us is perfect, but that's okay. Whatever *this* is has helped bring my smile back, and I thank you for that."

He warmed at the sentiment, and then, because he couldn't wait another minute, he tipped his head down and brushed her lips.

"Mmmm." He moaned as she opened her mouth to him, inviting his tongue. It felt like forever since they'd kissed like this. Something about being on what felt like the top of the world only added fuel to the fire.

Her arms coiled around his neck, and her fingers threaded into his hair, effectively holding him in place. But there was no place he'd rather be. Correction. He could think of a few other places more comfortable than that rock, but he'd take it.

She pressed her breasts against him, and he moaned again, remembering how they looked and felt in his hands and mouth.

He ran his hands up and down her back, but it wasn't enough. He slipped one hand under her top and relished the smooth, silky feel of her skin.

He could have stayed on that rock indefinitely but for the buzz of voices in the background. They reluctantly pulled apart, and he leaned his forehead against hers.

Panting, he whispered, "I want you so bad right now."

"I want you too."

"If only we could pull an invisibility cloak around us. I'd take you right here on this rock."

"Sounds uncomfortable yet oddly appealing."

He laughed and then kissed the tip of her nose.

"Would it be horrible if I said I'll be glad when my sister leaves? Don't get me wrong. I love her like crazy, but..."

"Her being here makes it hard for us to be together."

"It's hard, alright." He glanced down at the tent in his running shorts, and Callie followed suit.

"The big boy wants to come out and play," she said with a sexy smile.

Tracing her swollen lips with his thumb, he asked, "Do you want to play with me, Callie?"

He watched her squirm under his gaze, and she swallowed hard.

"More than I've wanted anything in a very long time."

He let out a breath. "How am I going to make it until tomorrow?"

She trailed a finger down the middle of his chest and peered up at him through dark lashes. "The anticipation will make it even sweeter."

"You think so, huh?"

She nodded. "It's times like this that I'm happy I have such an active imagination."

"I'm happy about that too," he said, wiggling his brows.

Loud voices made him glance over his shoulder. A group of people was lining up to jump off the cliff.

"We should probably head back. Miranda will be wondering what's taking me so long. Plus, she's anxious to spend the day with you."

Callie nodded, but then she leaned forward and gave him one more kiss, a G-rated one this time.

"What was that for?"

"For letting me vent and for just being you."

He stood up and gave her a hand off the rock. Once she'd hopped down, he entwined their fingers together, and they walked back to the resort hand in hand.

Since when do I get so excited about holding hands with a woman? You're such a wuss!

But he couldn't stop smiling, and he didn't want to. He loved the feel of her small hand in his, warm and strong yet vulnerable. He liked the idea of taking care of her—holding her, kissing her, feeding her, jumping off cliffs with her.

Jumping off cliffs. It seemed prophetic somehow. Wasn't that what he was doing, figuratively speaking? He was taking a risk for the first time since Cass. But he'd already determined that being with Cass hadn't been a true risk. She'd been a sure thing, at least in the beginning.

It was different with Callie. This felt real. This felt right. And it felt surprisingly like...forever.

Chapter 33

After a quick kiss goodbye, Callie and Chase went inside their separate units to change before spending the day together. And what a day it turned out to be! While they were kissing on the clifftop, Miranda planned a full itinerary, and when the three of them climbed into Chase's car, she laid it out for them.

"Did you know Waimea Canyon is called the Grand Canyon of the Pacific?"

"I read that," Callie said from the front seat.

Miranda had insisted Callie ride up front with Chase. It appeared that Miranda wasn't just a fan of her books but of her and Chase being together too. She could easily envision herself becoming friends with his sister. They shared a love of reading and also of Chase. *Wait a minute. What?*

"It says here..."

But Callie had zoned out. Did she *love* Chase? How was that even possible? She hadn't even known him that long. Sure, it happened like that in her books, but in real life?

At that exact moment, he smiled at her. Then he reached across the console, picked up her left hand, and entwined their fingers together. Such a simple gesture, yet it felt especially meaningful that he did so in front of his sister. It was like he was making a statement that they were indeed a couple.

Miranda continued from the backseat. "Let's stop in the town of Waimea and get lunch to take into the park."

"Um-hmm," Chase muttered.

Callie noted the look of exasperation on his handsome face.

"On the way back, I want to stop at this outdoor marketplace I read about. Supposedly, they sell quality handmade jewelry for low prices."

"Sounds perfect," Chase said with an eye roll.

Suddenly Miranda popped her head up from the travel guide she'd been looking at. "Are you being sarcastic right now?"

"Sarcastic? No. Not me."

Callie turned and gave Miranda an apologetic look. "I think it sounds like a wonderful day. Thanks for planning it."

Miranda beamed. "She writes the best romance books, *and* she's a genuinely nice person. You have to keep her, Chase."

While Callie appreciated the compliments, she stiffened at the reference to the future. She and Chase hadn't discussed that yet, and she waited to hear his response.

"I'd like to," he said and shot Callie a sweet smile.

She smiled back, though she wasn't sure how to take that. Had he meant, *I'd like to, but I can't? I'd like to, but I'm not committing to it?* What did it mean?

Miranda pressed on like nothing was amiss. "Mom would love her. Especially after what happened with Cassandra."

Chase stiffened. "Miranda..."

"Oops. Sorry. I assumed you already told her."

"Not everything, but now is not the time."

Callie assumed they were talking about his ex, but he'd never shared the details of their break-up. Then again, she hadn't told him the reason for her break-up with Adam either. Chase was right. They didn't need to be talking about this now.

Miranda seemed duly chastened, and the three of them were quiet for a while. Soon enough, they arrived at Waimea and sought out a sandwich shop. They bought drinks, sandwiches, and potato chips and then continued up the highway to the canyon.

The last time Callie had visited Kauai, her family hadn't explored the western side of the island, so this was all new to her. One of the things she loved about Kauai was the versatility of the landscape. There were lush green forests, sharp, towering cliffs, and beautiful sandy beaches. The island offered something for everyone.

The rest of the afternoon went as planned, with no further mention of exes or the future. They drove through the park, stopping at scenic overlooks and marveling at the beauty surrounding them.

They were also surrounded by chickens. They were everywhere—hens and roosters showing off their colorful plumage. They pecked the ground and happily accepted handouts from the tourists.

After eating lunch at a picnic table with a fantastic view of the canyon, they prepared to leave. Miranda had been snapping pictures with her phone throughout the day, and when they got back into the car, she showed some of them to Callie.

There were a couple of photos that gave her pause. "I didn't even know you took these."

"How could you? You two only had eyes for each other," Miranda said sweetly.

One picture was of Callie and Chase from behind. They were looking out at the canyon, and Chase's arms were fencing her in along the railing. Their heads were nestled together, and she was pointing to something in the distance. In another photo, they were facing each other, their profiles to the camera. They were smiling profusely, and Chase was tucking her windblown hair behind her ear.

Miranda had captured the moment perfectly in both shots. Studying them, Callie thought they looked like a real couple. In fact, she could envision either photo as a romance book cover, though she'd never put a picture of herself on the cover of one of her books.

Miranda tilted the camera toward Chase, and he took a quick look while he was driving.

"We look goooood." He'd purposely exaggerated the word good, and they all laughed.

"If you give me your phone number or email address, I'll send these to you," Miranda said to Callie. "Unless you'd rather not. You're probably not in the habit of handing out personal information to your fans."

What she'd said was true, but Callie had stopped thinking of Miranda as a fan and started thinking of her as a friend...or even a potential sister-in-law? *No. Don't go there.* But she would like to have the pictures even if they only ended up being part of her vacation memories.

"I'm not worried about you sharing it," Callie said and rattled off her phone number.

As Miranda was typing it in, Chase said, "No bugging her about when her next book is coming out and stuff like that."

"No worries. I can always find that out on Facebook, Instagram, and Twitter."

"You forgot about my website," Callie teased.

"Right. That too."

Chase shook his head, but he was smiling.

Before long, they'd arrived at the outdoor marketplace that Miranda had mentioned. There were rows of stalls set up with a view of the ocean in the background. Ordinarily, she'd have been excited to dig in; however, she was a bit distracted.

Chase had taken her hand the minute they'd stepped out of the car, and they slowly strolled along while Miranda excitedly ran up ahead and disappeared among the crowds.

"Do you think she wanted to give us time alone?" Callie asked.

"No. I think she's a shopaholic!" he replied with a laugh.

"I think your sister's great."

"I do too when she's not being a buttinski, which is most of the time."

"She loves you."

"I love her too."

He stopped in the middle of the row and glanced down at her. For a second, it almost felt like he'd said those words to her instead. *There goes my active imagination again.*

The moment passed when somebody accidentally bumped into them.

"We're right in the middle of traffic," she said.

"I was distracted."

Me too. Even though she was enjoying the day immensely, she couldn't stop thinking about when they'd get to be alone again.

They continued walking until Chase stopped in front of a stall with a display of sterling silver and gold jewelry displayed in glass cases.

If she'd been alone, she probably would have bought something by now. But she didn't mind window shopping, especially when she was on the arm of a handsome man like him.

Chase pointed at a gold necklace with a pendant depicting a hibiscus. The petals of the flower were hand-painted a brilliant blue, just like some of the hibiscus located right outside their doors at the resort.

"Do you like it?" he asked.

"It's gorgeous. Is it for your mom?" She assumed it would be since he and Miranda had discussed buying something for their mom at the market.

But he didn't reply. Instead, he motioned to the seller, a small Polynesian woman standing quietly nearby.

"Can we see this one, please?"

"Certainly," she said. She took the necklace out of the case and handed it to him.

Callie thought it was even more beautiful up close, but it wasn't her decision to make.

"Turn around," he said, surprising her.

"Me?"

He laughed. "Yes. I want to see how it looks on you."

The woman behind the case smiled, and Callie turned, lifting her hair so Chase could clasp the necklace. When she turned back to face him, he fingered the pendant, which felt cool against her warm skin.

"Beautiful," he whispered.

She wasn't sure if he meant the necklace, her, or both.

"Look in the mirror," the seller suggested.

There was a small standing mirror on top of the counter, and Callie leaned forward to look.

"It's fourteen-karat gold with hand enameling. Very pretty, yes?" said the seller.

Callie nodded.

"We'll take it," Chase said and whipped out his wallet.

"Would you like a box?"

"That won't be necessary. She'll wear it."

The woman told him the price, and he counted out the cash and handed it over.

"She's a very lucky lady," the seller said.

"I'm the lucky one," he replied, and taking Callie's hand, he led her away.

She fingered the necklace, in a state of shock. "But I thought this was for your mom."

"I never said that," he said with a teasing gleam in his eye.

"But you and Miranda talked about it..."

"Yes, and by now, she's probably bought several things for our mom. This one is for you."

"I don't know what to say except that I love it. Thank you."

"My pleasure."

She practically floated through the rest of the marketplace, stopping once to buy something for Quinn and her own mom. Finally, they met back up with Miranda, and as predicted, her arms were laden down with packages.

"Did you leave anything for the rest of the tourists?" Chase teased, relieving her of some of the bags.

"Very funny." Then Miranda's eyes went wide, and she reached out and touched Callie's pendant.

"Ohmigod. Where'd you find this? I love it!"

Callie looked up at Chase and saw he was grinning, which she took as permission to disclose the truth. "Your brother bought it for me."

Miranda glanced at Chase and then back at Callie. "You two are so stinkin' adorable together. You're just like a couple in one of your books!"

Callie flinched at that but quickly recovered. She hadn't had a chance to send Chase her rough draft yet, but she still planned on it. She hoped he'd find it just as "adorable" as Miranda surely would, but that remained to be seen.

"We're not that perfect, but close," Chase teased.

As they walked back to the car, he took her hand again, and she leaned into his side. No matter what happened from here on out, this had been a spectacular day, one she'd never forget.

While Miranda climbed into the back seat, Chase walked Callie around to the front passenger side. Before he opened the door, he put his lips to her ear and whispered, "I can't wait to see you in that necklace and nothing else."

If she'd thought the day had been perfect, the night would be even better...

Chapter 34

When they returned to the resort, a car was idling in front of their building. "Oh, my Uber is here," Miranda said.

Chase and Callie looked at her with surprise.

"Where are you going?" Chase asked.

"Home. Well, technically, not until tomorrow, but I decided to fly back to Oahu tonight since I have an early flight out in the morning."

"Why didn't you tell me? I would have driven you to the airport."

"It was a last-minute decision. Don't pretend you're upset about it." She gave him a knowing smirk.

The three of them stepped out of the car, and Miranda went over to talk to the Uber driver.

"Looks like we'll get to be alone sooner than we thought," Chase said.

Callie glanced up at him with a twinkle in her eye. "I'm going to miss her, though."

"Don't worry. I'm sure you'll see her again." The words slid out smooth as silk, and he really meant them. He didn't want this to be the end for them, and he hoped Callie agreed.

"Do you need help with your bags?" he asked when they caught up to Miranda.

"Yes, please."

Chase unlocked the front door, and Callie stood in front of her unit, looking uncertain. "Why don't you come inside so you can say goodbye to Miranda," he suggested.

She nodded and stepped in behind them. The next few minutes were a flurry of activity as Miranda gathered her bags and Chase helped carry them out to the Uber. Once the car was loaded, the three of them stood in a tight circle by the door, and he noticed Miranda's eyes looked watery.

"It was so wonderful to meet you," she said, throwing her arms around Callie and hugging her tightly.

"You too," Callie said with a big smile.

"You live in Michigan, right? But you never said where."

"She lives in Rochester," Chase interjected.

Miranda's eyes bulged. "That's practically right next door to us."

Callie giggled at her enthusiasm.

"We'll see each other again, then," Miranda stated with certainty.

"I hope so."

"You better go," Chase said, interrupting their mutual lovefest.

Miranda turned to leave, but he cleared his throat loudly and made her pause.

"No hug for me? I'm your blood relation, remember?"

They all laughed, and Miranda threw her arms around him and hugged him just as tightly.

"I love you, brother. Take good care of my friend."

"I will," he said. "Now, go."

Miranda hurried out the door, and he locked it behind her. When he turned around to face Callie, he saw her wiping away a tear.

"You okay?" he asked, coming to stand before her.

She nodded. "I'm so emotional today. Sorry."

"Don't apologize. Why don't we sit down?"

"Okay."

He took her hand and led her to the couch. Once they were seated, he gathered her close, and she leaned her head on his shoulder. "Want to talk about it?"

She took a moment to collect herself. "It's a combination of things, I guess. First, it was my grandma, and now your sister's leaving, and soon..."

He was smoothing his hand over her hair, and he paused. "Soon what?"

"Soon we'll be leaving too."

"We still have a couple of weeks left." After he said it, he knew it wasn't enough—for either of them.

"But before we know it, we'll be heading back to Michigan, and all this will just be a memory."

Placing his index finger under her chin, he tipped her face up. "Is that all you want it to be—a memory?"

She searched his eyes for a moment, and he wondered what she saw there. Knowing how observant she was, he guessed she saw a man who was in love with her.

She slowly shook her head, and he broke out in a smile.

"Me either." He dropped a kiss on her forehead. "I never expected this to happen, Callie. But now that it did, I'm not ready for it to end."

She sighed, and he felt her whole body relax in his arms. "I'm so glad I'm not the only one."

He considered picking her up and carrying her to his bedroom, but he had some more things to say to her first.

"Would you like something to drink? I've got wine."

"That sounds great."

He got up, and she started to follow him, but he motioned for her to stay put. "I'll get it. You just relax."

She smiled sweetly, and he went into the kitchen to pour their drinks. Truthfully, he'd needed a minute to compose himself after what they'd just shared. Was he getting in over his head? Was it too soon?

His hands were shaking when he poured the wine, and he spilled some on the counter. He couldn't remember ever being this nervous, even when he'd taken the bar exam!

It's not like you're getting married, you dufus. You're just admitting you'd like to see her when you get back home. No big deal. But somehow it felt like a very big deal.

He took a few deep breaths and returned to the living room with two glasses of wine. He noticed Callie had kicked off her shoes and was sitting with her legs curled underneath her. She'd worn shorts and a T-shirt for their outing, and her mostly bare tanned legs had been tempting him all day long. How he longed to run his hands up them, and then his tongue...

"Thanks," she said, eagerly accepting the glass of wine.

If he wasn't mistaken, she seemed a bit nervous too despite her casual pose.

They sipped in silence for a moment, and then he cleared his throat. "There are a few things I'd like to explain to you."

"Okay."

"First of all, about my ex…"

"You don't have to…"

"No. I want to, especially now that Miranda brought her up."

Callie nodded.

"She cheated on me with one of my best friends."

Callie looked pained as he continued.

"I caught them in the act one night when Cassandra was supposedly out with her girlfriends."

"You walked in on them?"

"Sort of. I went over to Patrick's house to hang out since Cass was busy. I heard some suspicious sounds, so I looked in his front window. Turns out she was *busy* doing him."

Callie's mouth made a big "O," and her forehead wrinkled in disgust.

"I felt like such a fool, you know? How could I have not seen the signs or suspected anything? I'm a divorce lawyer, for goodness' sake. I hear stories like that every day."

He'd tensed up at the recollection and took a deep drink of wine while he tried to calm down.

"The thing is, I've become jaded about relationships based on everything I've seen and heard, from my clients to what happened with Cass. To me, love is something that's destined to fail. It might start out with hearts and flowers, but inevitably it ends in pain and suffering." He paused to take a breath, and Callie jumped in.

"You must have examples of success stories too. What about your parents? Miranda said they're still crazy about each other."

"They're the exception."

"My parents are still together, and my grandparents were married for over fifty years. My grandpa passed away a few years ago, but my grandma loved him until the day she died."

Chase smiled at her earnestness. "I get it. You're an eternal optimist. You're a romance writer. You have to believe in love."

She shook her head vehemently. "You aren't the only one who was cheated on. It happened to me too. Only, I didn't see it with my own eyes—thank God. It started when I found a restaurant receipt in Adam's pants pocket to a place he said he'd never been before."

Chase bristled, the story already sounding familiar to him.

"When I questioned him, he admitted he'd been having an affair with a co-worker for months. Like you, I never suspected a thing. As a romance writer, I don't just write about hearts and flowers, Chase. I write about heartache and pain too, and I've experienced it firsthand. I know that not all love is meant to last. But I am an optimist, and I still believe in love. Do you want to know why?"

He had a feeling she was going to tell him no matter what, and he was rapt. "Tell me."

"Because even after what happened with Adam, I still have the desire to love and be loved. As long as my heart is beating, I know I'm capable of giving and receiving love. And in the end, that's all that really matters."

She looked like she was about to tear up again, and he couldn't take it. He didn't want to be responsible for bringing her more pain. He wanted to say that thanks to her, he was starting to feel capable of love again too. But something held him back.

"Come here," he said, holding out his arms. For now, he decided to go with actions instead of words.

She crawled onto his lap and buried her face in his neck.

He breathed her in, her scent becoming as familiar to him as his own. Despite his claim that he wouldn't fall in love again, he knew it was too late. She was in his arms and under his skin, and at that moment, he never wanted to let her go.

"Stay with me tonight," he whispered.

And she said, "Yes."

Chapter 35

Callie looped her arms around his neck, and he stood up and carried her to his room. This time, there was a sense of urgency as he tumbled onto the bed with her and immediately claimed her lips. She felt it too, and she clutched his shoulders, pressing her body tightly to his. She needed this, needed him, and she had no intention of holding back.

She tasted the wine on his tongue while his hands started tugging up her shirt. Then his warm palms were on her abdomen, sliding upward until he cupped her breasts. She moaned against his lips, and she felt him smile.

In the meantime, she'd slipped a hand under his shirt and was caressing his chest. She heard his sharp intake of breath as her hand drifted lower, her fingertips teasing him above the waistband of his shorts.

He broke the kiss just when she was about to unbutton them. "Arms up," he demanded, eyes ablaze.

She immediately complied, and he whipped off her T-shirt in one fluid motion. His eyes drifted over her face and down to her breasts, where her nipples were poking against her bra, demanding to be released. Spotting the front hook, Chase smiled and quickly clicked it open, revealing her breasts to his heated gaze.

He didn't even bother removing it. He simply pushed the bra cups aside and dipped his head down to draw her right nipple deep into his mouth. She shoved her hands in his hair and held him in place while he nibbled, licked, and teased her into a frenzy, and then he repeated the sweet torture on her left breast.

Heat pooled between her legs, and she squeezed them together to relieve the ache. Her head lolled back, and Chase gently pushed on her shoulders to get her to lie on her back. Then he began licking a path down the middle of her chest to the waistband of her shorts.

He unbuttoned and unzipped them in a flash and began sliding them down her legs, taking her panties along for the ride and then tossing them off the bed. She glanced down and watched as he slowly slid back up her body and then nudged her legs apart.

"Beautiful," he whispered before his head disappeared between her legs.

She practically bucked off the bed, arching her hips to meet his tongue. "Chase..."

Gripping her hips to keep her in place, he feasted on her like a starving man at a buffet.

He brought her to the brink of ecstasy, and then suddenly he pulled away and rolled off to the side.

"What...?"

He grinned. "Don't move."

Like she was going anywhere! Before she knew it, he was naked, sheathed, and crawling back over her. She eagerly reached for his erection, gliding her hand up and down his hard length.

"Need inside you," he said gruffly.

She nodded and guided him to her entrance. At this point, she was so worked up she could hardly wait for him to fill her. But he seemed intent on drawing it out—inching forward and then withdrawing until she was writhing with need.

He was keeping most of his weight off her, and she watched his arm muscles bulge with the effort.

"Watch us, Callie. Look at me loving you."

Loving me? Does he realize what he just said? But his eyes were focused south, and he continued teasing her, slowly lifting both of them to the height of pleasure. Their bodies were slick with sweat, and she grabbed onto his hips, her eyes following the path of his movements.

The next time he slid forward, she cried out. "Chase..."

"Tell me. Tell me what you need."

"I need more. I need...you!"

His head popped up, and their eyes caught and held. At that moment, she saw everything in stark relief. It was like the whole room was lit up even though it was pitch black. She saw him gazing down at her, his eyes brimming with emotion, and she felt her own fill with tears.

He brought a hand up and cupped her cheek. "Callie," he whispered.

"I know."

And then they both let go. All their physical and emotional longing was laid bare as they reached the peak together amidst a hailstorm of moans and sighs.

He kept moving until they were completely drained. Then he gently rolled them to their sides and held her close as their breathing evened out and the sweat dried on their skin.

Callie was afraid to move and break the spell that cocooned them. Right then they were the only two people in the world, and everything was perfect.

Chase lay still, his eyes closed and his chest rising and falling with every breath. She studied him, committing every nuance of his gorgeous face to memory. This time, though, it wasn't for her book. It was for her own personal story. Even if she never saw him again, she'd always remember this moment.

Then his eyes popped open, and he smiled at her. "Hey."

"Hey."

"I thought you might have fallen asleep."

He shook his head. Then he took her left hand and placed it over his heart. "Feel that?"

She nodded, his heart pounding beneath her fingers.

"I was worried I was having a heart attack," he said with a grin.

"Don't joke about that. It happens."

"I know, and now I understand why."

She had a feeling he was about to tell her something important but didn't know how. "We're pretty good together, huh?" she prompted.

"Pretty good? That's the understatement of the year."

She laughed and placed a kiss on his chin. "They say vacation sex is the best. Maybe that's why."

He shook his head. "I think this would happen anywhere with you." He leaned forward and softly kissed her lips.

They were quiet for a few beats, and then he said, "Callie?"

"Yeah?"

"I'd like to continue seeing you when we get back to Michigan."

She glanced up at him and saw uncertainty etched on his beautiful face. Was he afraid she'd say no? "I'd like that too." She'd hoped to dispel his concern, but his brow was still furrowed.

He was obviously still grappling with something, but she didn't want to push. He'd already said more than she'd expected, and for now, it was enough.

"I just don't know..." he began.

She shifted to her side. "You don't have to make any promises, Chase. You don't owe me anything."

"But..."

"Neither of us expected this, and I get that you need time to process it."

He shoved a hand through his hair, looking frustrated. She was a word person and could easily express her thoughts in words and sentences. But she understood that not everybody operated that way. Chase was obviously struggling to define his feelings, and she accepted that. But maybe she needed to convince him without words.

"Chase?"

"Yeah?"

"Why don't you dispose of the raincoat," she said, glancing downward.

He chuckled. "Be right back."

She admired his backside as he strolled into the bathroom. Once he'd closed the door, she moved to sit on the side of the bed, still naked. She took a few deep breaths as she waited for him to come out.

A few minutes later, he emerged, looking surprised to see her sitting there.

"I thought you'd be dressed," he said, his eyes roaming over her naked body.

She shook her head. "Come here."

His eyes blazed at her command. He stepped closer but paused just out of reach.

"Closer." Her voice shook a bit because, up until now, he'd been the one in charge. But the change-up was obviously welcome...

He stepped forward, his erection at full staff. He cupped her face and tilted her head up. "You don't have to..."

"I want to. Let me."

She didn't wait for his reply. She simply wrapped her hands around his manhood and brought it to her mouth. She remembered what he'd said earlier: "Look at me loving you." She wanted to say the same to him, but her mouth was a bit...full.

It didn't matter because he was watching her intently, his hands buried in her hair as she sucked him in deep.

"Callie…"

She was a woman on a mission, and she would not be deterred. The laser focus she applied to her work, she now applied to pleasuring him. She employed every technique from every women's magazine article she'd ever read on the subject, and she was rewarded with enthusiastic groans and sighs.

It wasn't long before he shouted, "Coming!" If it was meant as a warning, she didn't heed it. She kept working him until she'd wrung out every drop of pleasure. When she finally released him, he looked at her like he'd never seen her before.

"Did I surprise you again?" she teased.

"Always."

Always. She liked the sound of that.

Chapter 36

Chase had it bad. After spending the past few days wrapped up in Callie's arms, he'd had to give her up, and he was already missing her. Callie's friend Quinn had come to visit, and Callie had left his bed earlier that morning to meet her at the airport.

He'd offered to accompany her, but she'd declined, promising they'd get together while Quinn was there so she could introduce them. While he was honored that she wanted him to meet her best friend, all he could think about was how their time was running out. They only had ten days left on the island, and he wanted to spend them with her—alone.

He chided himself for being selfish, especially since Callie had been so accommodating when his sister had come to visit. But a lot had changed since then. He and

Callie had hardly been apart since Miranda had left, and he'd been loving every minute of it.

The first time Callie had spent the night, he could hardly wait for her to awaken the next morning. He'd lain on his side and watched her sleep, her eyelids fluttering and a slight smile on her face like she was having a good dream.

She'd been wearing one of his white T-shirts with nothing underneath, and when she shifted to face him, he saw the distinct outline of her nipples through the material. He resisted the urge to reach out and touch her since they'd stayed up late the night before and she probably needed rest. But she moved again, and the sheet dipped down to expose the tops of her bare thighs.

This time, he couldn't resist. He gently grazed his fingertips up one thigh and down the other, reveling in the feel of her smooth, warm skin.

Then he softly brushed her lips with his. Her eyes popped open, and she gave him a sleepy smile.

"Morning," he said, his voice thick with desire.

She laid a hand on his bare chest. "Mmm. Morning."

"Didn't think you were ever gonna wake up."

"I was dreaming."

"What about?"

"You. Us."

He scooted closer so their hips were aligned, and she wriggled against his erection. "Details, please."

"It's kind of fuzzy. But you were caressing my thigh, gliding your finger up and down but stopping short of..."

"Like this?" He repeated what he'd done a minute ago, and she sighed.

"Yes."

"Then what?"

"Then you kissed me, but it was so light and gentle I barely felt it."

"Like this?" He brushed his lips over hers with a bit more pressure this time.

"Um-hmm."

"Then what?"

"Then my nipples tightened under your T-shirt, and you stared at them and licked your lips."

"I did? In the dream, I mean?" He was beginning to wonder...

"Yes. You looked like you wanted to ravish me in my sleep."

He finally caught on, and he threw an arm around her waist and pulled her closer.

"Good one. You had me going for a minute there."

"I don't know what you're talking about," she teased, feigning innocence.

"That was no dream. I did all those things while I was waiting for you to wake up."

"Why didn't you keep going?"

"I was trying to be patient, seeing as we just made love a few hours ago."

"Patience is overrated." With that, she reached between them and cupped him over his boxer briefs.

"I'm glad we agree," he said and rolled her over on top of him.

After making love that morning, they'd gone on to spend the next two days and nights together. In between all the sex, they walked the beach, swam in the pool, took a late-night hot tub, talked, laughed, and generally enjoyed each other's company. They separated for a couple of hours each afternoon so Callie could write and he could pretend to do some work, but he couldn't wait until they came back together again.

They also ate every meal together, taking turns cooking until they'd run out of food, and finally, they were forced to go out to dinner or starve.

It was at the restaurant that she told him about Quinn coming to visit.

"That was kind of short notice, don't you think?" he said, realizing his mistake right after he said it.

"You mean like when Miranda came to visit?" she replied pointedly.

"You're right. Sorry."

"She'll only be here for a few days. Then she's flying to L.A. to visit her cousin."

He pushed away his selfish thoughts and spent the rest of the time asking questions about Quinn.

But Callie wasn't fooled, and on the drive home, she said, "What's wrong?"

"Nothing."

"You've hardly said a word since we left the restaurant."

He glanced over at her and sighed. Ever since they'd shared their secrets, he couldn't seem to keep anything from her. "It's stupid."

"Try me."

"I'm going to miss you while you're with Quinn."

She smiled big. "You are?"

"Um-hmm. I might not be able to sleep without you next to me."

She laughed. "We haven't exactly slept much."

"You know what I mean."

"We still have tonight and after she leaves."

Neither of them had talked much about going home even though it was lurking in the background. Everything had been so wonderful the last bunch of days, and it was hard to think about returning to his "real life." But soon enough, he'd be up to his eyeballs in legal documents and meetings, and she'd be busy too, and they'd have to make a concerted effort to see each other. Here, they lived right next door. Hell, they'd practically moved in together.

But this vacation bubble they'd been living in was about to burst, and he wondered where that would leave them.

That night he made love to her with an intensity that surprised them both. It was almost like he was never going to see her again. Afterward she lay sated in his arms, and he almost said the words he'd been holding back for the past three days. They were right there on the tip of his tongue, but he wasn't sure the timing was right.

He didn't want to spill his guts and then not be able to see her, touch her, or talk to her while Quinn was there. So, he'd decided to wait. If Callie noticed anything was amiss, she didn't comment. She simply curled into his side and fell asleep with her head on his shoulder. Trusting, caring, beautiful Callie—the woman he loved.

Chapter 37

Callie's book was three-quarters of the way finished, and she was anxious to share it with the world. But first, she wanted to share it with him—her muse and the man she'd fallen head over heels in love with.

She didn't have much time before she had to meet Quinn at the Kauai Airport, but she wanted to send him her draft before she left. Over the past few days, she'd come up with a book title and sought out a cover photo. Finding a cover photo that accurately embodied her story was one of the most challenging and enjoyable aspects of her job.

She wouldn't share the cover with Chase until her graphic designer had finalized it, but she hoped he'd understand why she'd chosen it and wouldn't be too jealous. The cover model was a handsome, shirtless man with dazzling green eyes that resembled Chase's, and that was why she'd chosen it. Plus, there was a tropical scene in the background that reminded her of Hawaii. It was perfect.

Like she'd told him, she didn't usually share her first draft with anyone, so she hesitated for a moment, her fingers hovering over the keyboard. She closed her eyes and thought about Chase reading it and wondered what he'd think. Would he recognize himself right away? Would he be embarrassed? Flattered? Upset?

She was confident he'd like the sex scenes, but what about the scene where the heroine tells the hero how she really feels about him, and vice versa? Would the raw emotions make him uncomfortable? Would it prompt him to share his own feelings or scare him away?

Glancing at the time on her laptop, she had to decide. She couldn't sit there and guess at Chase's reaction any longer. If she took the risk, she'd have to deal with the consequences. If worse came to worst and he had a negative response, they'd never have to see each other again.

But the thought of that made her heart wrench. She couldn't imagine not seeing him, touching him, hearing his voice. He'd become as much a part of her as Kauai had. She'd never think of this place without thinking of him. True, she'd always have the memories, but that wouldn't be enough. She wanted more, and she hoped he did too.

"Just send it," she said. Her pointer was hovering over the send button, and suddenly she clicked it, the sound like a gun blast in the quiet room.

Then she quickly shut down her laptop, picked up her purse, and left the condo, resisting the urge to tell him she was leaving. She'd already said a long goodbye earlier and promised to introduce him to Quinn during her stay.

A short time later, Quinn raced toward her in the airport with arms flung wide and a bright smile on her pretty face. They hugged each other tight, and then Quinn pulled back and eyed her closely.

"You look...different."

"I'm not sure how to take that," Callie teased.

"I mean it in the best way. You look healthier and more vibrant than when you left home."

"It's probably the sun." Callie flapped her hand dismissively. "I was pale as a ghost in Michigan."

Quinn shook her head, her silky blonde hair brushing her shoulders. "Nope. That's not it. There's something else..."

"Fine, I'll admit it. I gained a few pounds. I forgot how delicious the food was here."

Quinn laughed. "You look great. You needed to put on some weight after..."

"Let's not talk about sad things, okay? You're here, and I'm so excited. I've missed you." With that, Callie grabbed Quinn's hand and led her to the baggage claim.

"Sorry I can't stay longer, but I only get so much time off, and I promised I'd visit my cousin too."

"It's okay," Callie replied, and she meant it. She loved having Quinn there, but after she left, she'd still have Chase. At least, she hoped so.

As if Quinn had read her mind, she said, "So, what's the latest with Chase? We haven't talked much in the past few days."

That's because I've been rolling around in his bed. "I know, but we'll have plenty of time to catch up. Let's get your bags and get out of here."

She managed to hold Quinn off until they stopped for lunch at a nearby deli.

"I'm not letting you off the hook. Spill," Quinn said after they'd placed their orders.

Callie took a deep breath. She wasn't sure where to start. This was her best friend, but she wanted to keep some of the intimate details about Chase to herself. On the other hand, outside of her family, Quinn knew her better than anyone. Even if she didn't spill all, Quinn would be able to read between the lines.

"I'm in love with him," Callie blurted out.

Quinn's gorgeous blue eyes went wide. "In *love* with him?"

Callie nodded. "Big time."

"Wow!"

"I know. Crazy, right?"

"Why crazy?"

Callie shrugged. "One, we haven't known each other that long. Two, I came here to write, not fall in love. Three, he's a divorce lawyer, for Pete's sake. Four—"

"Stop right there," Quinn said, holding up her hand and laughing. "What's wrong with him being a divorce lawyer?"

"Hello? Could we be any more opposite? A divorce lawyer and a romance writer? It sounds ridiculous."

"Opposites attract," Quinn stated simply.

"Yes, and they also end up in divorce court just like Chase's clients."

"As opposed to, let's say, you and Adam, who were more alike?"

Callie flinched.

"Sorry, sweetie, but it's true. You and Adam may have been more compatible on paper, but look what he did to you."

"I guess that just proves it can happen to anyone."

"There's no magic formula for love. Surely, you know that."

Callie sighed. "I'm scared, Quinn."

Quinn immediately reached out and clasped her hand on the table. "I get it. I do. You didn't expect this to happen, and I'm sure he didn't either. But it did. So, what are you going to do about it?"

Just then the waitress came over with their food, which saved Callie from having to answer. They each took a couple of bites of their sandwiches before she replied.

"I kind of already did something."

"You told him you're in love with him?"

"Not in so many words. Well, sort of."

Quinn furrowed her brow. "You lost me."

"I let my book heroine speak for me."

She watched while Quinn deciphered her words.

"I sent him the first draft of my new book, which is essentially about us with a hefty dose of fiction thrown in."

"But you never let anyone read your drafts."

"Exactly."

Quinn sat back in her chair, looking shocked.

Callie took a few more bites of sandwich because, despite feeling anxious about what she'd done, she was starved.

"Well, what do you think?" she finally said.

"I hardly recognize you. First, you jump off a cliff, literally, and then you jump again, figuratively. I love the new you!"

"Thanks?"

Quinn laughed. "When did you send it to him?"

"This morning, before I came to pick you up."

"How do you think he'll react?"

"I'm not sure. That's what I'm worried about."

"I can't wait to meet him."

"I promise I'll introduce you, but not yet. You're only here for a little while, and I want to hang out with you. What should we do today?"

"Beach, shopping, dinner, meet Chase. In that order."

Callie giggled. "You're not going to let this go, are you?"

Quinn shook her head. "I'm dying to meet the man who stole my best friend's heart. I need to make sure he's solid."

Callie smiled, knowing that Quinn only wanted the best for her. "Fine. We'll do things your way, but I have a few rules before you meet him."

Quinn rolled her eyes. "Of course you do."

"One, no telling him embarrassing stories from my past. Two, no grilling him about his job or his exes. And three, no asking him his intentions for the future."

Quinn shook her head. "Do you really think I would do that?"

"Just covering all the bases."

"Don't worry. I won't embarrass you. I promise."

Chapter 38

The receptionist at Edwards, Stewart, and Wineman answered with her usual politeness.

"Hello, Jessica. It's Chase. Is my dad around?"

"Hold on, Chase. Let me check."

While he was on hold, he paced back and forth across the small living room, practicing what he wanted to say. He'd given it a lot of thought, and he felt certain about his decision. His only concern was how his dad would react to the news.

A minute later, Daniel Edwards came on the line. "Hello, son. How's Hawaii?"

"Just like you'd expect. The weather's been great, hardly a cloud in the sky."

"Don't rub it in. Your mother's been begging me to take her there again. Speaking of your mother, she's anxious for you to come home."

Chase smiled, thinking it was typical of his dad to defer to his mom on all things emotional. He'd bet that his dad missed him too, but he wouldn't dare admit it.

"I'll be home soon." *Sooner than I'd like.*

"I'm guessing you didn't call just to update me on the weather. What's on your mind?"

Chase covered the phone and inhaled deeply. He'd imagined this could go one of two ways. Either his dad would be understanding or he'd tell him no. If it was the latter, Chase had already decided he'd head out on his own. He had plenty of experience and an excellent reputation in the community. It might take a while, but he'd find a way to make it work.

"I've been doing a lot of thinking since I've been gone."

"And?"

"And I'd like to transition into another area of family law within the practice if that's acceptable." He felt like a teenager asking to borrow the car.

"Another area?"

"Yes. I'm burnt out on divorce law. I want to switch it up, maybe move into estate planning."

"But we have Bob for estate planning."

"Bob's been talking about retiring soon."

"He's been saying that for the past ten years."

"Well, maybe I can take some of his workload. He can show me the ropes before he leaves."

Daniel gave a weary sigh. He probably needed some time to absorb the news, and Chase would give him that. "You don't have to answer right away, but when I get home, I'd like us to sit down and discuss it."

"We'd have to run it by the team too."

"I understand that."

"Can I ask you a personal question?"

Uh-oh. Where's he going? "Okay."

"Does this have anything to do with that woman Cassandra?"

"Cass? No. Why?"

"Well, I know she did a number on you, and you haven't been yourself since."

Funny, but he hadn't thought much about Cass since he'd been gone, and especially since Callie...

"Listen, son. We all suffer setbacks. That doesn't mean you have to uproot your entire life. You're a damn good divorce attorney."

"I can be a damn good estate planner too."

"You might find it boring."

"I doubt it. For once, I'd like to practice law with people who aren't hell-bent on destroying each other."

"That happens in all areas of the law. It's the nature of the beast. But if you're really serious about this..."

"I am."

"Then we'll discuss it further when you get back. In the meantime, I'll mention it to Bob and see what he says."

Chase stopped pacing and stood at the patio door, looking out at the ocean. "You sure you're okay with this?"

"I kind of have to be, don't I? You're my son, and I want you on my team. So, if that's what it takes…"

For some reason, Chase got choked up. "Thanks, Dad."

"You can thank me by coming home and getting your mother off my back."

Chase laughed because everyone knew that despite his grumbling, Daniel adored his wife.

"Oh, and bring the new girl around. Callie, is it? Miranda told us all about her at dinner the other night."

Of course, she did. "Um…I don't know, Dad."

"What don't you know? Miranda said you were crazy about her."

"Miranda has a big mouth."

Daniel chuckled. "Anyway, I have to go. My next appointment's here."

After a quick goodbye, Chase hung up, feeling a mixture of relief and trepidation. Daniel had taken the news better than he'd thought, which was great. But when he'd mentioned meeting Callie, Chase had balked.

While he wanted to continue a relationship with her in Michigan, he wasn't sure he was ready for all that went with it. Meeting the parents was a serious step in his mind, and he wasn't sure that either of them was ready for that.

Damn if he hadn't thought about her all day long though. He hadn't heard her come back yet, and he assumed she and Quinn were still out exploring the island.

He hoped to see her later, but for now, he decided to head to the pool. He took his phone so he wouldn't miss her call and chided himself for acting like a lovesick fool.

Once he'd claimed a chair poolside, he settled in and decided to check his email before taking a swim. He skimmed down through the various work emails and advertisements until he saw Callie's name, and he broke out in a huge grin.

In the subject line, she'd typed *Chasing Forever* with a heart next to it. She'd said she would send her draft to him, but he was still surprised. Noticing the time stamp on the email, he realized she'd sent it this morning before leaving to pick up Quinn from the airport.

It meant a lot to him that she'd sent it, since she'd never shared her first drafts with anyone before. Her email read:

Chase,

Here's the first draft of my new book. I'll be editing it multiple times before it ever sees the light of day. I hope you enjoy reading it, and feel free to share your criticisms with me. I can take it! I'll be anxious to hear what you think. Talk soon.

Callie

Chase clicked on the attachment to download her draft, leaned back in the lounge chair, and began to read...

Chapter 39

Callie kept checking her phone throughout the day, but she hadn't heard from Chase. She and Quinn had done all the things on Quinn's list, and now they were driving back to the resort after having dinner at Puka Dog. Callie smiled, thinking how much had changed since she'd first eaten there. That time, she'd been spying on her muse, and now she'd fallen in love with him. Had he read her draft yet? Had he figured out he was her hero?

"Just call him," Quinn said when they were driving away.

"I can't."

"Why not?"

"What if he hated it? What if that's why he hasn't contacted me today? He's had plenty of time to read it by now."

"Maybe he hasn't checked his email. Maybe he's been moping around the resort, missing you the way you've been missing him."

"I have not been moping."

Quinn laughed. "You've been doing a good job of trying to hide it, but I can see right through you."

Callie sighed. "I promised I'd introduce you, but maybe we should wait until tomorrow."

Quinn shook her head. "Uh-uh. You are not backing out of this."

"But..."

"No buts, Callie. We're going inside to freshen up, and then you're taking me next door to meet the man."

Callie took a deep breath. "You're right. I jumped off a cliff, so I can do this."

"That's my girl!"

When she pulled into the parking lot of the resort, she looked around furtively for Chase's car. She didn't admit to Quinn that for a second, she'd hoped he wasn't there. But his SUV sat in the same parking space as when she'd left that morning. Had he stayed there all day? Was he waiting for her?

Callie and Quinn went inside, Quinn rolling her suitcase behind her.

"I forgot how gorgeous this place was," Quinn said, stopping to sniff the hibiscus that was growing outside

Callie's door. Then she glanced at Chase's front door and back at Callie. "He literally lives right next door. How convenient!"

"Shhh! He might be able to hear you."

Quinn laughed while Callie hurriedly unlocked her door and stepped inside. The sun was already starting its descent and it cast an ethereal light through the windows.

"Your room is right down the hall," Callie said, pointing.

"I remember. I'll be ready in a few minutes."

But will I? Callie pulled out her phone again. Nothing.

She went into her bedroom to change from the shorts and tank top she'd worn all day into a sundress she'd bought that afternoon. Thanks to Quinn, this dress was by far the sexiest one she had. The background color was a beautiful shade of blue with a smattering of large pink flowers on it. But what made it sexy was the low neckline and the open back. The color did wonders for her skin tone and perfectly matched the pendant Chase had given her. By the time she'd fixed her hair and touched up her makeup, she felt like a million bucks. She slipped on her wedge sandals and went back to the living room to wait for Quinn.

But Quinn was already there, standing in the center of the room and looking out the window. Callie assumed she was admiring the view, but when she followed the path of Quinn's gaze, she froze.

There was Chase, hands in the pockets of his cargo shorts, presumably watching the sunset. Since his back was to her, she couldn't see his expression, but his shoulders looked tight, his stance pensive.

Her nerves shot up a notch, and she wanted to slink out of sight. But then, as if he'd sensed her presence, he turned and looked right at her.

"C'mon, Cal. It's time," Quinn urged.

Swallowing hard, Callie realized she had no choice. Quinn was already moving toward the patio door, and Callie followed on wooden legs.

Quinn gave her a reassuring nod and stepped aside to let Callie open the door and go out first. The breeze was warm, and the sky was lit up behind Chase's fine form. Their eyes met, and he smiled softly.

"You look beautiful," he said on a whisper.

She was immediately flooded with warmth and relief. "Thank you."

"Ahem," Quinn inserted.

For a second, Callie had forgotten Quinn was standing there. Embarrassed, she quickly made the introductions. "Chase Edwards, meet my best friend, Quinn Larson."

They shook hands, and Quinn gave him the once-over. "Callie's told me all about you," she said with a knowing smile.

"Uh-oh," Chase replied with a charming smile of his own.

Quinn giggled. "All good."

"Whew!" he said, pretending to wipe sweat off his brow.

Callie watched their interaction with a twinge of jealousy. Not because she thought they were flirting with each other, but because of the ease with which they carried themselves. She could take a lesson from them. Then again, maybe she was being too hard on herself.

She'd accomplished a lot since coming to Kauai, including writing a new book, jumping off a cliff, wearing a bikini and sexy sundresses...and perhaps the most courageous thing of all—falling in love.

"Looks like a beautiful sunset tonight. You arrived at the perfect time," Chase said congenially.

"I was here with Callie and her family before," Quinn said. "The sunset is even more spectacular from the beach."

"We could all walk down there," he offered.

Callie appreciated that he was trying to include Quinn, though she was anxious to be alone with him.

Quinn glanced over at her and said, "You know what? I'm kind of tired from traveling. Why don't you and Callie go ahead?"

"Are you sure?" Callie and Chase said at the same time.

They all laughed.

"I'm positive. It was very nice meeting you, Chase."

"You too."

Quinn turned and wiggled her brows at Callie before disappearing inside.

Chase immediately held out his hand to her, and she took it, eager for his touch. He clasped her hand tightly as they walked across the lawn to the path that led to the beach.

"I'm kind of overdressed for this," she said self-consciously.

He shook his head. "You look perfect."

If she wasn't mistaken, his voice sounded gravelly, and he seemed more subdued than usual. She was dying to ask him if he'd read her draft, but she decided to wait. It was a beautiful night, and she was determined to enjoy the sunset, if nothing else.

When they reached the end of the cement path where it met the sand, Chase let go of her hand to remove his shoes, and she did the same, although she'd liked the extra height her sandals afforded.

There were already several people lining the beach to watch Mother Nature's display, but Chase led her to a quiet area apart from the crowd.

"Here okay?"

She nodded, her throat too constricted for words.

He stood behind her and slipped his arms around her waist, hugging her back to his front. She leaned against him, happily soaking up his solid warmth.

This reminded her of the first time they'd watched the sunset together, when they'd shared their first kiss. The start of it all...

"Callie?"

"Yes?"

She was grateful at that moment that he couldn't see the fear in her eyes. She focused on the sunset, watching it slowly sink into the horizon, which was as far and wide as the eye could see.

"It's us, isn't it? In your book."

Before she could answer, he turned her around to face him and locked his arms around her back.

She looked into those enchanting green eyes and slowly nodded.

"I loved it," he said. "Every minute of it. I couldn't put it down. Didn't want to."

Why did she get the feeling that he was talking about more than just her book?

She released a long breath. "Thank God. I was…worried."

"About what?" he asked, smoothing the back of his hand over her cheek.

"I don't know. Everything. I didn't want you to be mad that I'd used you as my muse."

"How could I be mad? You made me out to be perfect!"

She laughed. "Creative license."

"I'm not, though."

She slid her hands up his chest and entwined them behind his neck. "You are to me."

He dipped his head down and kissed her, long and slow just like the first time. She forgot all about the sunset, the crowded beach, and everything else. There was only this, only them—her muse, her hero, her love.

Finally, they came up for air, smiling at each other like lovers do. But was that all they were?

"There was one chapter in particular that stood out," he said, his eyes sparkling in the twilight.

"Let me guess. The one where they had sex for the first time."

"Nope."

Her eyebrows shot up. "No?"

He shook his head. "It was further along in the story."

Callie sucked in a breath, afraid to believe she knew what chapter he was referring to.

Chase placed his index finger under her chin and tipped her head up. Pinning her with his gaze, he said, "It was when they said, 'I love you,' for the first time."

"Ohhh…" She assumed the sun had completely sunk into the ocean because she felt a chill wash over her.

"You captured the moment just right. I believe they were on a beach just like this."

She nodded, mesmerized by his words, the way he was looking at her, and his hand pressing into her lower back.

"The hero, Chad, looked into Cassie's eyes and told her he loved her and that he couldn't imagine his life without her."

"You memorized it?"

He nodded. "I can relate. I came to this island looking for something, but I didn't know what it was until I found you. And now I can't imagine my life without you in it. I love you, Callie."

Thank goodness he was holding her up; otherwise, she might have collapsed on the sand. She stood there, staring at him, absorbing the words and trying not to cry.

"I believe this is the part in the book where the heroine tells the hero she loves him too," Chase prompted.

"Ohmigod. I'm so sorry," she said, finally coming around. "I love you too! And I'm so glad you feel the same. Otherwise, I would be seriously mortified right now!"

He tipped back his head and laughed loud and long. They were virtually alone now that night had fallen, and only a few stragglers were left further down the beach.

"Kiss me again," she said once he'd stopped laughing.

"Gladly."

This time, he hauled her into his arms, leaning back so her feet came off the ground. They kissed like nobody was watching, and afterward, when he set her back down, they were both breathing hard.

"We should probably head back, even though I'm not ready to leave you," she said.

"It's only temporary. After Quinn leaves, I'm not letting you out of my sight."

"I like the sound of that."

He took her hand, and they slowly walked back up the path to their condos. They paused outside her patio door, reluctant to part.

"I wish I knew how your story ends."

Smiling up at him, she replied, "I'll let you read it when it's finished, but I guarantee there'll be a happy ending."

Epilogue

One Year Later

Chase practically dragged Callie up the trail to the clifftop. She'd been fighting him every step of the way, but he was determined to get her there.

"I'm not jumping. I did it once, and I don't need to do it again!"

He didn't reply. He just smiled and shook his head. He could hardly believe a year had passed since they'd been there.

All his fears about what would happen after they'd returned to their "real lives" had been unfounded. They no longer lived next door to each other, but a fifteen-minute drive turned out to be nothing. They'd easily slipped into a routine of seeing each other after work and sometimes during the middle of the day.

Callie would surprise him by showing up at his office with lunch or dragging him off to a restaurant, insisting he needed a break. Now that he'd transitioned into estate planning, he hadn't felt the same need for a break, but he loved seeing her just the same.

And so did everyone else at the office. She'd effectively charmed everyone there, including his sometimes-reticent father. Don't even get him started about his mom and sister. They were over the moon that Callie had joined their family, even though she hadn't *officially* joined them yet. But he hoped that was about to change...

He'd brought her back to Kauai under the pretense that they needed a winter getaway, and where better than the place they'd originally met? This time, things were different, though. They only rented one condo instead of two, and he'd chosen the same unit she'd stayed at before in reverence to her grandmother's memory.

Callie had cried when he'd told her, but he knew they were happy tears. They were excited to return to Hawaii even though they were only staying for a week this time.

They both had busy schedules, especially now that her book, *Chasing Forever*, had hit the bestseller list. After their trip, Callie would begin a book-signing tour, starting in Michigan and then fanning out to a few nearby states. He'd been so proud of her the day she'd told him the news. Of course, he was proud of her every day. Her writing had flourished this past year, and she was getting ready to release another book soon.

When they reached the clifftop, Chase walked right past the group of teenagers waiting to jump and led her to the outcrop where he'd found her talking to her grandma last year.

"What are you up to?" she said as he helped her up on a rock.

"Sit down," he replied, trying to keep his voice steady. He wanted this to be perfect, but he was sweating from the climb, and his hands were shaking. So much for being the perfect book hero!

She sat on the rock and scooted over to make room for him, but he remained standing.

"Chase?"

She looked so beautiful sitting there in the sunlight and so much happier than when he'd found her there the last time. He'd like to think he was partially responsible for that, especially since she'd had the same effect on him.

"I didn't bring you up here to jump this time," he began.

She looked somewhat relieved, but her brow was furrowed with confusion. He wasn't one for long speeches unless he was in a courtroom and it was required of him. But he wanted this moment to be memorable, and he searched for the perfect words.

Callie was the wordsmith, though, not him. Realizing she wouldn't expect that of him, he dropped to one knee.

Her hands automatically flew to her mouth, and her brown eyes went wide. "Ohmigod."

"Callie?" He fumbled around in his swim trunks pocket for the box. He'd worn a swimsuit to throw her off and had no intention of actually swimming.

"Yes!"

It sounded more like an answer than a question, but he continued just to be sure.

"I brought you here because this is where it all began for us. This is where I fell in love with you—your beauty, your caring nature, your humor. I want us to come back here every year for the rest of our lives. Will you marry me?"

She cried and nodded as he finally freed the velvet box from his pocket and popped open the lid.

Miranda had insisted on approving the ring before he bought it, and judging by the way Callie was gazing at it through her tears, he felt assured it was the right choice.

"Ohmigod. Yes!" She held out her left hand, which was shaking.

He slipped the ring on her finger, and then she flung herself into his arms, almost toppling them both off the rocks.

"I love you, I love you, I love you," she repeated, plastering his face with kisses.

Then there was loud cheering, and he remembered they weren't alone. Some of the people waiting to jump had obviously caught on to what was happening, and they were smiling and clapping.

Chase gave them a wave of acknowledgment while Callie held up her hand with the ring. Another round of cheering ensued, and then the onlookers went back to their purpose for being there.

"You planned this all along," she accused, her smile bright and her tears now gone.

"Guilty as charged."

"I thought you came up here to jump again."

"I did, but not off this cliff. We took a risk a year ago by falling in love. Now we're taking another risk, and I'm ready for it—ready to be your husband and love you for the rest of our lives."

She leaned forward and kissed him, sealing the deal with her lips and effectively telling him everything he wanted to know. But he should have realized she'd back up her actions with words.

Chasing Forever

"Now you know the end of the story. I told you there'd be a happy ending!"

THE END

Stay tuned for book two of the Sweet Escapes series, a new standalone vacation romance coming soon.

Author's Note

I hope you enjoyed *Chasing Forever* and will take a moment to leave a review on Amazon and/or Goodreads. While you're there, check out my other sweet and sexy contemporary romance novels.

I love to connect with readers! Please visit my website, and follow me on Facebook, Instagram, and Twitter.

Thanks for reading!

Susan

https://www.susancoventry.org

https://www.facebook.com/authorsusancoventry/

https://instagram.com/susancoventryauthor

https://twitter.com/CoventrySusan

https://www.amazon.com/Susan-Coventry

https://www.goodreads.com/author/show/14930782.Susan_Coventry

Made in the USA
Columbia, SC
23 October 2023

24832683R00202